THE TOLWORTH BEACON

Huw Langridge

The characters and events portrayed in this book are fictitious. Any similarity to real persons, living or dead, is coincidental and not intended by the author.

Cover design by: Katarina

ASIN: B0876GKRFN
ISBN: 9798646781551

For Martha

CONTENTS

PROLOGUE

She'd been in there, and everyone had waited.

It had been dry and warm outside when she'd arrived last night at sunset, when the neon lights were welcoming those who were going to spend their Saturday night dancing and drinking and making memories. She had felt energised after the private flight from her Inverness keynote address, ducking under the helicopter blades on the high roof of the building, being met by her team, preparing for a long night of work.

Now, this morning, three of them were riding the lift down to street level to answer questions. The greyish blue light of a cloudy dawn had begun to alter the tone of the London cityscape beyond the glass. She could see it had rained hard in the dark hours. Fast rivers were running down the outside of the windows.

Three human reflections. She looked at her own shape, tired, shoulders forward, gently rocking one arm of the eye-glasses between her fingers.

Looking down she could see the streets. At ground level, the slowly changing traffic lights, reflected in shimmering semi-circular curbside puddles. Lonely, with fewer cars to command. Small details reaching her. Pinpoints of immediacy in the fleeting canvas of the night's tapestry, a fabric faded by long hours of delicate work.

She took a deep breath as the lift slowed to the ground floor. She lifted her shoulders and turned around. Brushed chrome doors slid open to expose them to the bright fluorescent lobby.

Then she could see people. A lot of them. So many more there than she'd expected. Flashing lights. She blinked a few times and took a few steps forward. Almost immediately a microphone found its way to her, held by a news reporter.

She opened her mouth to speak.

MONDAY

A loud bang dragged me backwards out of sleep. I don't know why but the first thing I thought had happened was that something heavy like a chopping board had fallen off one of the kitchen worktops; the impact had a particular reverberation. But what followed was talking, and it wasn't in the flat, it was outside in the road. Another repeated bang like the one that had woken me, and I knew what it was. A car door closed definitively by someone who wasn't planning to go back and check they'd done it properly.

I had to remind myself that Steph wasn't lying next to me on my right, her usual undulating shape in the bed, one leg under the covers, one leg on top, breathing slowly and heavily through a relaxed throat.

Of course, she wasn't there. She wasn't bloody there. She wasn't there, and that was how sleep bewildered you.

There wasn't a lot of light in the room. Apart from the glow of my blue clock radio digits telling me it was 1:17am, there was an orange rhombus slanted across the opposite wall, a reflection cast by the streetlight where the top of the curtains failed to completely join when I drew them before getting into bed a couple of hours earlier.

I got up, parted one curtain a little and looked down to the road.

Our flat was on the first floor, with an entrance via outside steps on the left side of the block. There was no front garden to speak of. The lady downstairs had invited us for Christmas drinks one Boxing Day. Having people walk right past her window on the pavement outside during the day in a way that made it feel like they were in her lounge, was more than Steph and I would be prepared to tolerate. We had the choice at the time, so we took the upstairs one. The bedroom of this flat, number 25b, looked down onto Wellowteme Crescent and a triangle junction with Chalkweald Avenue; the triangle itself little more than a raised patch of grass with a faded yellow gritter box on it. As I examined the view I was expecting to see the results of a car collision. I should have known better, because if anyone knew what a car crash sounded like it was me.

There had been a few dings out there in the seven years we'd lived on Wellowteme Crescent. At least two a year. Most recently a young lad in a Honda Civic not slowing down enough for the junction had clipped the back end of a Citroen C1 driven by an older lady who had the right of way. The problem was the faded paint markings, which regularly caught out the uninitiated. Three winters ago, a guy rolled his van over the grass triangle. Ironically there was black ice and he was going way too fast, and he obliterated the gritter box. The fire brigade had to cut him out of the van. He lost a leg I think. Was another life being turned upside down this very moment?

I couldn't tell for sure, but there didn't seem to be any evidence of a crash.

What I *could* see was a police car parked over to the right, across the drive of a house across the road. I was pretty sure it was number twenty-two. The house was on a diagonal as it also overlooked the triangle junction. The police wagon wasn't on flashing lights, but its engine was still running. Had it not been the height of summer I would have been able to see all the action through the deciduous oak tree on this side of the road. But with the full foliage in the way I couldn't. Through the slightly swaying tree I could see the movement of three or four people on the pavement, and heard little more than the sound of voices, but I was unable to make out what anyone was saying.

A lady appeared, crossing the road, briefly illuminated by the headlights of the police car. She was probably in her thirties. Short bleach blonde hair with dark roots. Arms crossed, cigarette between her fingers. She was wearing a sky-blue onesie.

I'd earlier folded my white t-shirt and jeans on the bedroom chest of drawers. I put them on and went down the hallway, past the front door and into the living room to find my shoes. I was pretty sure I'd kicked them off by the coffee table when I sat down to do the jigsaw earlier. I flicked the wall light switch and regretted its cold brightness immediately as it forced my eyes closed. I switched it off again and moved over to a smaller free-standing lamp in the corner near the television. With a warmer light on I caught sight of the puzzle. Partially completed. Five-hundred pieces. It was practically all white, except for a few black marks which I had yet to slot into the middle (I always started with the edges). I was a fanatic, but this jigsaw was definitely among the oddest of all the ones I had done.

I found my shoes, where I thought they'd be, wedged under the coffee table. Badly scuffed black slip-ons that I'd used for work until they were no longer worthy of being seen with a suit and were now only used for non-official duties. Things were not normally left on the floor, and certainly not under Steph's watch, but blokes were more likely to let it slide. Despite the frustration I would also feel when constantly picking up toys off the floor, I still desperately missed encountering the remnants of Freya's five-year old imagination. Dolls arranged in strange poses by the bathroom door with their clothes on back to front. Tetris-like Lego Duplo constructions littering the kitchen linoleum. It had only been, what, two weeks? But it felt like two months, and I was pretty sure I would still feel as empty when two months finally did come around.

Not bothering about socks, I sat on the sofa and slipped on the shoes. I felt smelly and unwashed and unpresentable, but still I grabbed my house keys off the table and walked down the hall to unlock the front door. Outside was an immediate right turn and a set of concrete steps, fifteen of them, down to the path that ran along the side of the building to the road. Heading down the steps I could hear more voices now, bouncing off the walls between this block and the one next door.

There had been no other cars at this time of night. Our little road, Wellowteme Crescent, was usually pretty quiet, even in the day. There were some cars parked along the kerb, including my own humble black Vauxhall Corsa, and as I cut in front of mine and crossed the street I got a better picture of the event that had woken me.

It was a warm night in early July, and the sky was clear but a little hazy. A slightly yellow full moon had edged west across the sky above the houses, making a silhouette of the large antenna on top of the roof of number twenty-two. I walked towards the three people standing by the police car. The officer was tall and thin, towering over the man he was talking to, and as I got closer I realised I knew who the shorter man was. The shape of his bald head gave it away. It wasn't the owner of number twenty-two, as I'd expected, even though the door to that house was open and all the downstairs lights were on. The man on the street talking to the policeman was none other than my Stock Room Supervisor from Hollyways, the branch of supermarket chain in town where I was the Store Manager. The two of them, plus the lady in the onesie had been talking but they stopped and looked at me as I drew near.

'Is that you Eamonn?' I said.

He looked at me. A moment of coalescence of thought crossed his eyes and then he smiled. 'Hello Chris. Of course, that's your place over there isn't it?'

'What's going on? Is everything ok?'

Eamonn Daly had dressed for the warm night. He was wearing a plain dark vest, cropped camouflage trousers and black Converse trainers, and when I got close enough to him I could smell his body-odour mixed in with a musty after-shave that was probably lingering on the clothes rather than him. He gestured his thumb towards number twenty-two, 'There's been a break in.'

'An attempted break in,' said the officer.

'I heard someone rattling a door,' said the lady. 'Sounded like the back door. It woke me up. Went on for a good few minutes. I called 999.'

'Can I ask where you live?' said the officer.

A female officer emerged from the open front door, clicked on a torch and started to walk around the side of the house, aiming the beam of light down at the slate path.

'I'm there,' I said, pointing back through the oak tree. 'First floor. Number twenty-five. Twenty-five B.'

Eamonn said, 'I was about halfway along Chalkweald Avenue. I'm looking after a friend's dog while they're away. A lovely whippet called Jackson. I'd been walking him up at Tilmere Woods because I realised as I was about to go to bed that I hadn't taken him out for a walk this evening.' He twisted and pointed behind him. 'Anyway, as we came toward the junction I saw the police car parked up here. I came over to see what was going on.'

'Did you happen to see anything from where you were?' the officer asked me, turning the volume down on a hip radio that was squawking chatter at no one in particular.

I shrugged. 'I was asleep. First thing I heard was a car door. Probably yours officer. Is Malcolm ok?'

'You didn't hear the rattling?'

'To be honest,' I said, 'you might be better off checking with the people on Copsgate Avenue. That's the road behind Malcolm's house. If it *was* the back door, any sound would be more likely to travel in that direction.'

'Well *I* heard it,' said the lady, looking at me, 'and I live next door to your block, on this side.' She was indicating the building to the left of mine which, granted, was nearer to number twenty-two.

'Did you see anyone?' I asked her.

She took a quick drag of her cigarette and blew it into the air, shaking her head.

Addressing Eamonn and the lady in the onesie, the officer said. 'I'll need to take your details, so we can give you a call if any other activity is reported.'

The lady nodded, and the officer took notes as she gave her

name, address and number.

Eamonn and I also gave the officer our details.

Speaking to Eamonn, the officer said, 'I was wondering where I'd seen you before. You work at Hollyways don't you?'

'And so does he,' said Eamonn, putting his hand on my shoulder.

'My wife shops there, she loves it,' the officer said to me.

'Well I'm very glad to hear it.'

'Are you looking forward to Saturday then?' The officer asked me. 'Some of us are assigned to crowd control.'

'There's a lot to organise,' I said. But whether I was looking forward to it? That depended on which way the wind was blowing.

The female officer appeared from beside the house and walked up to us. She switched off her torch and clipped it to her jacket.

'Well, the occupant, err Michael...' she removed a notepad from a pocket and started flicking through it.

'Malcolm,' I said. 'Renfield.'

'Yes Malcolm Renfield, said that nothing appears to be taken. There's no sign that the back door was even opened. Whoever it was must have been disturbed.'

'That door's locked anyway,' said Malcolm. No one had noticed him appear at the front of the house. His accent sounded like London. East end. This older man, who was probably in his sixties, with white hair, was wearing a black dressing gown. 'And the key's hidden in a jug in the dining room. Look, I know enough about police dramas to know you're not going to get any prints. It's a dry night so there won't be any convenient shoe marks on my back patio. I don't want to waste any more of anyone's time. Perhaps we can wrap all this up and go to bed.'

I didn't really know Malcolm much beyond the occasional friendly wave across the road. He was kind to Freya once. Gave her a quid for wheeling (more like dragging) his recycling bin out to the road one evening before bin day. I don't think he had any family, at least, not that I'd seen. I'd only ever spoken to him a couple times. I knew he was some sort of CB radio enthusiast and he had this big antenna on his roof.

I saw Malcolm was holding his car keys, he went over to his white Porsche Cayenne which was sitting in his drive. He remote-unlocked it, and all the lights flashed, then he opened the passenger door, leaned inside, opened the glove compartment and emerged holding a thick, heavy black Mag-Lite torch. With everyone watching he brandished it above his head like an actor who'd just won his first Academy Award. 'I'm keeping this by my bed from now on.' And he started back towards the house.

'Well I'm gonna head off," said Eamonn. Got a big week ahead of us so I'd better try and get some kip. Lots to organise. Lots to... Calibrate!'

'Funny way to put it,' I said.

Eamonn smiled and shook his head in admission. 'It's late. I'm tired. I brought the dog out but I should have just gone to sleep. I guess I'll see you in a few hours.' He waved his hand towards number twenty-two and said to the officer. 'I'm glad all this turned out ok.'

'Goodnight,' the officer replied.

'See you at work,' I added.

Eamonn started off back along Chalkweald Avenue, the way he had come. I knew he lived about five roads away so had little more than fifteen minutes of walking ahead of him. Chalkweald wasn't such a big town.

The lady said. 'Well if you don't need me anymore officer I'm going to hit the hay.' She looked at her watch, 'Ten to two on a school night!'

And then it occurred to me. 'Where's this dog he was walking?'

'Oh,' the lady continued. 'Your friend said... he said his dog had probably gone off to find some bush to shit in. Said it catches up eventually.'

'Charming,' said Malcolm, still lingering by his front door. 'As long as it doesn't shit in one of *my* bushes.'

The officer said to the lady, 'Thank you for contacting us. And goodnight.'

She took that as permission to turn and head back across the road towards her building, pausing only to put the cigarette out on the ground with the sole of one of her slippers.

I wasn't completely sure, but I got the impression from the way Malcolm was loitering and not going back into his house that he wanted to say something to me but seemed to think better of it and went inside anyway. He *had* been looking at me though.

I said goodbye to the officers and crossed back to my flat. Ten minutes later I was back at my coffee table slotting a few more jigsaw pieces into their correct places. I'd finally started on the black bits.

Ten minutes after that I was back in bed, curtains fully drawn with no triangles of streetlight on the opposite wall. In the dark I was fighting to keep my eyes open. A strange way to spend a chunk of time in the early hours of a Monday morning, that had been.

I didn't see Eamonn at Hollyways initially when I arrived six hours later. This wasn't unusual. His shift started at six and I tended to reach my office by eight. The supermarket was on a retail park consisting of seven units, of which ours was the largest at fifty-five thousand square feet, dominating the entire north side of the square car park. Staff parking was down the side of the store in a different area from the main car park. Eamonn's metallic blue Peugeot was parked in its usual bay. I parked up and walked in through the goods entrance, said hello to Max, Eamonn's deputy, who was coordinating today's deliveries, and headed across the shop floor to my office, which was reachable through a door in one of the far corners near to the fish counter. And although I'd already had breakfast, the smell of baking bread never ceased to be intoxicating.

My phone pinged. It was a text from Valerie Lombardi from head office. We'd arranged for her to come the fifty miles from Salisbury for a meeting here at ten o'clock, plus a walk-around with Eamonn and Clem, my Deputy Manager. *Traffic bad, stopped for a coffee and a loo break. I set off early so should still make it on time.*

She ended up arriving at my office twenty minutes early. She was wearing a smart lime-green trouser suit and a small black canvas backpack on her back as she walked in (both straps on, even though she didn't hike here from Salisbury, she drove!). Her long curly hair was not completely under control. She had a Mediterranean skin tone and a slight Italian lilt to her voice. Valerie had been my direct manager at Head Office ever since I got the Manager role at this store, and she had been working for Hollyways for twelve years in total.

By ten o'clock the four of us were sitting in my office, Clem and Eamonn both wearing their purple Hollyways suits. I'd brought paper coffees from the machine in the staff room, and an open packet of Hollyways shortbread lay untouched in the middle of my desk.

Valerie was wobbling a pen between her fingers. 'So, we have a lot of things to cover this morning. Some of the planning I'll have to leave to you Chris and then I'll be back again on Thursday because Royalty Protection are coming at eleven that day and I want to be here for that. We'll be doing a bit of a dress rehearsal then, so we'll need a full staff meeting after lunch. Can we start with the theming?'

I leaned forward and consulted a printed spreadsheet on my desk. 'All the materials arrived last Thursday so that's the bunting, miles of the stuff. Pop-up stands, we've got twenty of those. Leaflets and the Anniversary Celebration Vouchers. One box containing five thousand leaflets and one box with a thousand of the vouchers. Three hundred A1 posters. Not sure we'll be using all of those to be honest. We've also got a hundred of those shoulder band things...'

'Sashes,' said Clem.

'Sashes,' I continued. 'In corporate purple with "Hollyways two-hundred" written on them.'

'The Pop-up stands. Are they different ones?'

Clem said. 'Yeah so we've got the "Your family partner for two hundred years" one. Ten of those. And ten of the standard one, you know the one with the mum in the car park. The bunting and the Pop-up stands are already up in the store. We did those on Saturday.'

'Great stuff. Any concerns at the moment?'

I looked at Eamonn and Clem for their take. Eamonn looked tired, not fully engaged. Neither of them said anything, so I said, 'I think we'll feel a lot better once we've done the walkaround with Royalty Protection. When we know where everyone needs to be.'

Valerie pulled a folder out of her backpack, which was no longer on her back, but beside her feet on the floor. She opened the folder and retrieved a sheet of A4, she handed it to me. 'This is the latest draft of the itinerary. Shall we run through it in situ?'

◆ ◆ ◆

'The Duchess's car is going to arrive here at nine-thirty,' said Valerie.

The four of us were standing outside the main entrance to the store. A few feet away, shoppers were noisily disconnecting and reconnecting trolleys from the stack. Valerie was pointing at an area with yellow cross-hatching painted on the tarmac, which was a pick-up and drop off point but not designed for parking.

'There will be two cars, but she'll be in the second one. Dame Hollyway will come in the first car and will greet the Duchess as she gets out of the second car and she'll walk with her into the lobby area to meet a couple of others. The CEO and his wife, the Mayor and the council leader. Also, Marianne. When we meet the Royalty Protection team later in the week we need to confirm how much of the lobby area needs to be cleared,' and now she was pointing at stock. 'Cos we've got those tidy tubs, the bottles of screen-wash and the bedding plant racks there. They might be in the way or restrict access because we'll have security people and all sorts coming through here as well. Not forgetting a wheelchair.'

My phone buzzed in my trouser pocket. I pulled it out and looked. It was from Steph. *Hi. Turns out I DO have to attend after all. Mum is with some friends up north for a couple of nights. Can you have Freya? Sorry!!*

Valerie was talking to Clem about the entrance doors. I waited for her to finish and then said, 'Do you mind if we take a short break. I could do with a visit to the gents.'

'Sure, let's meet back here in ten minutes. Can I get you a coffee from the machine?'

'Thanks.' I left the others and started walking along the central aisle in the direction of the toilets. About halfway down I overheard some women talking and caught the words "Wellowteme Crescent" being said. The conversation was taking place in the bread aisle. I slowed down, and turned down the adjacent aisle (Tea and Coffee) so I could eavesdrop on the women talking about my road. I started to tidy up boxes of tea on the shelf so as not to look to other shoppers like I was just gormlessly standing there.

'...It was his last job,' the woman continued. 'When he got home he told me. He was on duty with Ann McCarthy. You know Ann, don't you? Husband works in South Africa a lot. Apparently when Ann went into the house to interview him the man had hardly any furniture and he was listening to something weird on his radio. Like, all these numbers being read out.'

I remembered the officer had said last night that his wife shopped here.

'...He had all these papers strewn everywhere like he was decoding messages or something. She said it was proper weird. Apparently he's into all that CB radio stuff. Perhaps that's how they...'

'Help you find something sir?' Eamonn had somehow appeared next to me without me noticing, arms folded, a slightly smug look on his face like he'd caught me stealing or something.

'You creeping up on people now?' I said. 'I had a text from Steph. I was just working out how to respond. She was err... She was asking if I could collect Freya from school tomorrow and have her overnight. Steph's got to go to some property conference in Geneva.'

'What about her parents? Wouldn't she ask them before you?"

'It's just her Mum. But she's away tomorrow. Her Dad died before we met.'

'Oh, sorry mate. I didn't know that.'

I was scratching my head for no reason. Nerves probably, a little awkward talking about this stuff. 'Yeah, when she was nineteen. Some guy in his car texting his boss smashed into her Dad's car. This was before all the laws about phones and driving. Her Dad had forgotten to put his seatbelt on, which was unlike him apparently.'

'That's terrible to hear. How's it going with Steph? If you don't mind me asking.'

I couldn't hear the women in the next aisle anymore. Either they'd stopped talking or they'd carried on their gossip elsewhere. I was about to mention to Eamonn what I'd heard the women say just now about Malcolm and his radio, but instead I just answered his question. 'Bit of a shitshow to be honest. I'm trying not to think about it until after Saturday. I need to focus on this and not that, for now.'

Not taking my hint, he said, 'And how's Freya taking it?'

While he spoke, I was replying to Steph. *Don't apologise, she's our kid. Hope it goes well. Will you drop a bag over?* Then I hit SEND.

'She thinks it's temporary,' I said 'That Mummy and Daddy can't possibly want to do this for any longer than a few days. Like it's some sort of experiment, which I suppose it is.'

My phone buzzed. A reply from Steph. *Yes, I'll drop it over this afternoon. Thank you!*

Eamonn continued. 'She's five going on fifty that girl. You'll need to keep an eye on her. She's quite the little button.'

Eamonn was a single man. Ex-forces. I'd seen a picture blu-tacked to the inside of his work locker of him in full combat gear in the flat desert of Afghanistan, grinning, in what looked like brutal heat, wearing a camouflage cap to protect his bald head, and holding a rocket-propelled grenade launcher.

He and I had been work colleagues for three years now, and also friends. He was a good man. Solid and dependable, if a little black and white in his approach sometimes. It was Eamonn that recommended I went for the Store Manager role, a position I'd now had for eighteen months. I hadn't been planning to go for it, but I have Eamonn to thank for making me believe I could get it. He even took the time to give me interview practice. Rigged up a video camera in his flat to make the interview seem more "immediate", and offered to be another pair of eyes over my CV. He didn't need to do those things.

He put his hands in his purple trouser pockets, his bald head shiny under the supermarket fluorescents, which ever so slightly picked out the thin trail of a long scar across the right side. I'd never asked but I guessed it was a war injury. He carried on. 'Do you know what? If I ever have a girl I want to call her Grace. That was my Nan's name. And if I ever have a boy I'll call him Joshua. Joshua Daly. I had a buddy called Josh who we lost in a raid on our convoy, nine years ago now. And I always thought, you know... I always thought.' He put a hand on my shoulder and smiled, but it was a hollow smile. 'First, I have to find myself a wife, don't I?'

'You do! For no other reason that I still don't have a next of kin record for you in the HR system.'

'I'll email you one.'

It was still a blazing hot day when I left the office at six o'clock. I checked in with Eamonn before leaving, to ensure all was running smoothly out back.

I'd bagged a nice looking chicken and pasta salad in a plastic tub that had been marked down due to being on its use-by date. I also picked up a six pack of beers as I wasn't sure if there were any left in the fridge. The contrast of temperatures from inside the supermarket to outside was quite something. My car was hot and had that hot plastic smell. The steering wheel was uncomfortable to the touch. I wound down the windows and let what little breeze I could waft into the car as I navigated around the busy car park, past cars pumping out deep summer beats and people wearing the clothes they normally take on holiday. I drove home and as I parked outside my building I contemplated checking in on Malcolm. I thought better of it. The guy seemed to want to put a lid on the whole affair from last night, at least that was the impression I got.

The first thing I did when I got into my flat was change out of my work suit into shorts and a t-shirt, because I hated wearing my suit around the house, and because it was hot. I opened the windows in the kitchen and lounge wide to let in as much of the breeze as they would allow. I turned the chicken salad out onto a plate, got an ice-cold beer from the fridge (I had one left so didn't have to wait for the new ones to get cold). I sat myself down at the coffee table in the lounge and looked at the jigsaw. I had probably fewer than 50 pieces left to slot in.

I'm a member of a rather obscure Facebook Group called the Jigsaw Collective. There are thirty-six members. Anyone can join, but we don't get many requests from people. The main reason being that because the rules are laid out for anyone to see, it puts most people off. The group is not for everyone.

The members are based all across the UK. This sounds more complicated than it is, but these rules evolved over the four years we've been doing it, so it's second nature to those of us who crafted them. Once a month each member pays two pounds to enter, or you can pay in bulk in advance. We transfer the money into a bank account belonging to the group admin and treasurer, whose name was Mike Allman, also known as Mike the Vault. Once we're enrolled for the month and we're given the go-ahead from Mike, we start by selecting the most complicated or challenging jigsaw we can find. Mike the Vault picks everyone's names out of a hat, records the names in column A on a spreadsheet, then picks everyone's names again, and records each one in column B. Off that list we are then contacted by Mike with the name and address of the person whose name is in column B where our name is in column A. Like an elaborate Secret Santa. We then send the jigsaw we've selected to the member of the group we have been allocated on Mike's sheet.

We send the jigsaw by Recorded Delivery to arrive with the

recipient on the first Saturday of the month (in this case two days ago). Everyone gets their jigsaw at the same time. At midday, (if you were participating) you would post a photo of your newly opened jigsaw on the Jigsaw Collective Facebook group, with all the pieces in a jumble, and the BBC News channel in the background so everyone knew that the time you took the photo was legit. Following that, the first member of the team to post an image of their completed jigsaw puzzle would win the monthly prize. The prize, we had all agreed some time ago when we hit thirty members, was a case of wine, paid for with the collected entry fees, sourced at cost by Mike the Vault who originally suggested it because he worked at a wine distribution company.

I have to say I was a little surprised about the jigsaw I had been given this month. I've had jigsaws that were all one colour before but there had been chatter on the group for some months that people had become a bit tired of receiving them. It was a bit of a cop out. Mind you, this one did have this intriguing section of what looked like black writing in the middle, so there was clearly more to it that just a single colour, even if the writing only took up about ten percent of the overall image. So, I set about completing it, eating the occasional fork of chicken salad, staring out of the window at slowly reddening evening and sipping beer, which was going down extremely nicely in this heat thank-you-very-much.

The only time I ever won the challenge was the previous November. I had been sent a four-thousand-piece puzzle. The picture was a beautiful photo of the very last stages of a sunset, with the only distinguishing feature being a couple of noctilucent clouds kissing the stratosphere, so high that they were still lit by the sun. I was staggered that I won given the size of the jigsaw, but I'd had nothing else to do that weekend as Steph had taken Freya to York to visit some University friends. After each challenge is over we all get to find out who sent us our jigsaw. The sunset photo had actually been taken by the guy who sent me my jigsaw, he'd had his picture custom made into a puzzle. The wine went down very well that Christmas.

On this current jigsaw I'd been working my way from the

border towards the middle over the last couple of days, and it took me about thirty or forty minutes to get the last of it done. I knew I'd lost the challenge, as one of the other members had already posted a picture of their jigsaw on Sunday morning, so I hadn't been too bothered about rushing it. Some of the other guys and girls in the group deliberately cancelled everything in their diaries for the first Saturday of the month purely so they could hit the jigsaw hard, get it finished, and win the kudos, which was more important to most of us than the prize.

I slotted the last piece of the puzzle in at about a quarter to nine, ran my hand over the smooth completed work in satisfaction (I always do that) and then I really took in what the picture was.

All the jigsaws I had ever given or received as part of the Jigsaw Collective had come in a box, with a picture on the front. This one didn't, and that's why I hadn't known what the puzzle picture was, until now.

On the white background, the black writing spelled out in a functional font:

15733khz.

Now, I didn't know much about what I was looking at, but I knew that "khz" stood for kilohertz, and what I was looking at was a radio frequency. Judging by the numbers I knew it wasn't an FM frequency, more like shortwave.

I laughed because it seemed absurd, and the sound of my laughter in the slowly darkening flat was also absurd. It was as if a member of the Jigsaw Collective was trying to send me a message, telling me to listen to a specific radio station. I knew I had a DAB radio in the kitchen and I was pretty sure that digital radios didn't pick up shortwave. I wasn't even sure if I had an older radio that might... but then... Hang on. I did, didn't I?

Being the top floor flat we had access to the attic. Steph and I had stored a few boxes up there when we moved in. This was seven years ago but I knew we had an old painting radio in one of those boxes. At least I was pretty sure we still had it. Older gadgets tended to last forever, unlike the newer stuff.

I went to the kitchen cupboard to retrieve the attic hatch release pole and went into the hallway to open the hatch. The pole also hooked into a ladder which pulled out and slid down enabling access to the roof space.

I climbed up the ladder, the metal rungs cold under my bare feet. Although the space up there was quite large (if a little short on headroom, making it more of a crawlspace) the total area stretched to the whole size of the flat. Only a small area around the hatch had been boarded with plywood in order for it to take any weight. It was surprisingly dust free up there. We'd stored five boxes on the plywood boards and they all bore the same UKSTOR BEST REMOVALS branding on the side. Steph had ordered a bulk delivery of boxes from UKSTOR when we moved, and these ones didn't have any room designation or other distinguishing description scrawled on them like the others had. My feet were beginning to complain about carrying my weight on the thin rungs of the ladder, so I brought all five down to the hall rather than fishing around in them up there.

The first box I opened contained three box files containing all our conveyancing and mortgage documents from the last house move, and bank statements and bills from our last place. Looking at the correspondence there was something strange about the wording of our old address. So common then but so alien now. A distant time that preceded Freya making a mark on our world. A time when Steph and I did things for ourselves first, when we had time to appreciate each other as lovers.

The second UKSTOR box contained the radio I was looking for. I knew we'd kept it. A very old small black one that belonged to my parents, given to me along with a load of other stuff when they both moved to Perth, Australia, to live down in Freemantle with a group of retiree friends all seeking a new lease of life in the sun. They all moved out there together eight years ago. Now the whole group runs a charter boat company taking tourists out to Rottnest Island. Not something I'd ever thought they'd do in their sixties.

The radio was about half the size of a shoebox, splattered with various flecks of paint. Duck egg blue from the old bedroom, the colour we'd painted it about a month before our wedding day. Lime green from the spare bedroom, painted about six months earlier in the space of one day because her Mum was coming to stay, and we'd had an allergic reaction to the magnolia room we'd inherited from the previous occupants. It had been a nice little flat in a different, cheaper, area of Chalkweald, but the kitchen and lounge were too small, and we knew we wanted kids, and then I got the Deputy Manager role at Hollyways, and things moved fairly quickly after that.

We were moving up the property ladder slowly. Our plan had been to sell this one in a couple of years and move to a three-bedroom house, once we'd paid off a bit of the mortgage on this flat and put ourselves in a position to have a decent deposit on a bigger place. With Steph and Freya camping out at Steph's Mum's place, that plan was currently on hold, along with any plans to create an occupant for that potential third bedroom.

I checked that the painting radio had the shortwave band, and it did. The partly scratched off text that said AM/SW/FM was written across the front, and the radio had one of those small plastic windows and a thin red needle that that moved across the band as you twiddled the knob. The ON/VOL knob was next to the tuning knob. I turned it. Apart from a tiny click, nothing happened. There was a figure of eight power socket in the back but no power lead. I slid open the battery cover. It took two large cylindrical C type batteries. The two that were in there had become oxidised with age, the flaky white dust staining my fingers as I prized them out.

I went to the kitchen drawer to see if I had any replacements, although I already knew that I didn't. AAs and AAAs in abundance, for various remote controls, and toys of Freya's, but no type C's.

Keeping the radio out, I returned the boxes to the attic, put the ladder back up and closed the hatch, tiny flecks of white paint dropping from around the hatch as I pushed it closed.

Hollyways sells batteries. I looked at my watch. It was almost nine-thirty. We close at nine. The only other place that would be open at this time of night would be the petrol garage, but it was seven miles away. I'd had two beers, so driving was out of the question. The batteries would have to wait until tomorrow.

I stared again at the jigsaw, the floating black letters. Functional information against a stark white backdrop. Obviously, I'd lost the jigsaw challenge, so there was no need post an image to claim a win, but despite that I picked up my mobile phone and snapped a picture of the completed puzzle. I was about to hit the share button to upload the image to the Jigsaw Collective Facebook group, but for some reason I found myself hesitating. I don't know why, but something deep down was telling me not to do it, not to press that button. Instead, I deleted the image and put my phone back down on the coffee table. An odd sensation came across me, as though my phone had somehow become contaminated by having a picture of the jigsaw on it. I went into the kitchen and detached a yellow sticky note from the pad on the side and wrote down the frequency numbers. Then I crumpled the jigsaw down, collapsing the pieces and pulling them apart. The wrecking of it was compelling, satisfying. The undoing of all that hard work. Deconstructing something that had taken so long, and so much work to build. Like a marriage.

I placed the pieces back into the ziplock sandwich bag they had arrived in. Going into the kitchen once more I went to the bin and fished the brown jiffy bag the jigsaw was sent in to see if there was any clue as to who had sent it to me.

The address label for Chris Powell, 25b Wellowteme Crescent had been printed by a computer and the sender's name was not written anywhere on the package. The postmark was smudged. The anonymity was part of the rules while the game was still going on. No clues to be found there then. If I wanted to find out who sent me the puzzle, there was only one thing I needed to do.

TUESDAY

I got up at six o'clock and cleared last night's dumped shorts and t-shirt off the floordrobe and put them in the wash basket. The warm July sun was rising into a beautifully clear sky. We were getting a real run of cracking weather. Rare for a British summer. A swallow was chirping loudly outside my bedroom window.

While I was waiting for the coffee machine to finish dribbling into a cup, I sent a Facebook direct message to Mike the Vault to ask him which member of the group he had picked out to provide me with my jigsaw challenge. I could see he'd been offline for eight hours, so I needed to wait for him to wake up before I'd get a response.

After breakfast (two chocolate croissants) I drove down to Hollyways and went straight to the aisle with the batteries. The supermarket was busy. It had been open for an hour by then, but it soon filled up. I picked up two packs of Type C batteries and handed them, and a tenner, to Amy, one of the till ladies, and asked her to run it through for me. I knew I'd have to come back to the tills later because I had to sort something out for dinner for Freya's upcoming overnight stay, so I told Amy I'd pick them up later.

I found Eamonn just inside the front entrance speaking to Clem and pointing at the doors, so I went over to see what that was about. When he saw me Eamonn said, 'Morning Chris, we were just talking about Valerie's suggestion about where the barriers should go inside the shop. Because we want to create a better path for the Duchess to come through and get to where we're going to unveil the plaque which is over there by the wall. Valerie says it should go straight there so the walk is more direct, but I was just talking to the Clem here and I think he agrees with my suggestion that it should take a more curved route. It would show off more of the store for the television and allow us to bring more invited guests in because there'll be more pathway for us to line with people. Don't you reckon so Clem?'

'Eamonn,' I said. 'Who put twenty pence in you?'

He smiled, 'Huh, twenty pence? Sorry, I was rambling, but don't you think it's a good idea?'

'It's not bad actually,' said Clem.

I became aware of an old lady hovering near the fruit section clearly eavesdropping on our conversation. I didn't really want to get into a disagreement with Eamonn at the entrance to the supermarket with members of the public in earshot, so I employed the simple management technique of starting to walk somewhere with the intention that the other person would follow. It worked. In fact, they both followed.

I considered Eamonn's idea for a moment and then said 'It's a good suggestion. I'll take it back to Valerie as ultimately, it's her decision. But why are you worrying about it? She was pretty clear about where she wanted the barriers to go, and I'm sure I heard something about the measurements of the path having to tally with the number of guests we're bringing in to ensure that we don't overcrowd the space.' We arbitrarily came to a stop at the end of the kitchenware aisle, surrounded by cutlery, cooking knives, plates and bowls.

'But maybe we could get some of the staff's family members in. You could bring Steph and Freya. Others could too. It might give us space for an extra twenty or so. Where are you going to be standing again?' said Eamonn.

'Clem and I will be over by the plaque when the unveiling happens. There'll be a few of us over there and all the Hollyways top brass, lined up next to it.'

I found myself looking closely at Eamonn's eyes. 'What's this all about? Are you wanting to ask me about your own proximity to the proceedings?'

Eamonn shook his head vigorously. 'No, no, not at all. No, I just want to make sure you get the right level of recognition here. You deserve it after you were so instrumental in upping the financial turnover of this branch. What with it being the flagship store and everything. And it seems only right that more family members can join in the festivities.'

Clem said, 'Should we really be planning on changing the routing plans that have been in place for months? Plans that involve going against Valerie's directions from yesterday? I'm not sure how well that would go down Chris. Sorry Eamonn.'

Eamonn considered this for a moment and then nodded, 'You're right Clem. Changing things at the last minute might not achieve anything useful. Chris, I don't want to put you in an awkward position.'

I watched him for a moment. I knew he was playing the reverse psychology card and damn it, it was working. Because his idea made a lot of sense.

My phone pinged. Not a text ping, a Facebook notification ping. I pulled it out of my pocket. A message from Mike the Vault which read: *Hi Chris. Bit of a weird one this. Got time for a WhatsApp?*

'Everything ok?' said Eamonn. From the corner of my eye I could see he was trying to look at the message on my phone.

Looking up at him I instinctively angled the phone towards my chest and said, 'Yes it's nothing. Ok look. I'll call Valerie, see what she says about your idea.'

'Only if you want to, mate.'

I walked back to my office and placed a call to Valerie. I got her voicemail, so I left a message for her to call me. Then I initiated a video-chat with Mike the Vault on WhatsApp. He answered almost straight away, his face occupying my mobile phone screen, made orb-like by the front facing lens of his phone camera. His receding hairline looked even more receded. He was in his garden.

'Working from home today?' I said.

'Yeah. I got a Wi-Fi extender to stretch as far as the deck. I'm getting some much-needed vitamin D. I've picked up a summer cold and we've got this policy now where we stay away from the office, so we don't spread it. Costs the company to have staff off sick, but now we just work from home. Anyway. Yeah, like I said it's a bit of a weird one this.'

'How so?'

'OK so your jigsaw was sent to you by the new guy. David Wenlock. He joined the group three weeks ago if you remember, and this was his first challenge entry. When I was putting together the sender's list last Monday he sent me a direct message asking if he could have you as his "challengee", if that's even a word. Said he knew you in real life and wanted to play an "in joke" on you by sending you a specific jigsaw. It was a break from the norm. I don't normally do that. I usually keep the selection process totally random, but I didn't see any harm in it as a one-off, so I put his name against you. I hope it was worth it. So, what was it?'

'What was what?'

'What was the jigsaw?'

Thinking quickly, I said, 'Oh… it was a… picture of our school. We went to school together.'

I'd hated what I'd said as soon as I'd said it. I hated myself for not telling the truth to Mike, who I'd known through the group for four years. All for what? A liar like David Wenlock, whoever the hell *he* was? But if the mysterious David Wenlock could spin a yarn to engineer a situation, then I was going to play him at his own game. Except it didn't work out like that because Mike the Vault then said, 'But the thing that makes this all so weird is that he's now left the group. I went to message him today to see if everything was alright, you know, to find out why he left, but he's no longer on Facebook. He basically quit Facebook in between receiving your address from me last week, and this morning.'

My desk phone started to ring. Mike was still talking. 'I

searched for him a few times to make sure. But it's true. He's done a complete disappearing act. Is that someone trying to ring you?'

'Yes, sorry I've got to go. But thanks for getting back to me about this. I'll track... old Dave... down.'

I closed the WhatsApp call and picked up my desk phone.

'Hi Chris. I got your message.' It was Valerie.

'Oh hi, thanks for coming back so quickly.' I explained Eamonn's idea about the entrance pathway for the Duchess, and how we would get family members of staff in lining the walkway if we curved it slightly past the fruit and veg section.

'It's not a bad idea, that,' she said. 'Why didn't he mention it yesterday?'

'Maybe he didn't think of it. None of us did.'

'I don't know how the guy from Royalty Protection will feel about last-minute changes but if I get Dame Hollyway on side she should be able to swing it with the powers that be. I'll send it up the chain here.'

And that was that. Either they accepted it and Eamonn would be pleased, or they would reject it and Eamonn would be satisfied that I'd at least tried. Still, I did wonder why he was so hung up about it.

Valerie called me twenty minutes later.

'We're doing it.'

'That's great.'

'Dame Hollyway has approved it so if you can get an email out this afternoon to staff for them to give us names of anyone they want to bring as guests then they must respond to me by close of play today and I'll get the list pulled together and sent off first thing. They have to vet all the names you see.'

'I'll do that now.'

I was on the last push to get out of the office and pick up Freya from school. I cursed myself for leaving it so late, but I was working on the email Valerie had asked me to send out to the staff. I had to pick up Freya at ten past three. It was five to, and the drive was ten minutes away. But then I remembered that I hadn't got the bloody food. I needed to find something not too nutritionally vacant. I ran onto the shop floor and over to the Italian ready-meals aisle, panic-bought a lasagne for two, a bag of salad, and a garlic bread. I also got some apple juice and some ice-cream. My last stop was the toy aisle to pick up a Kyoot Spighdaz Blind Bag, a "collect them all" toy that comes in a foil wrapper meaning you don't know which one you'll get. I knew she loved them. After I paid for everything I retrieved the batteries which I had asked Amy on the tills to run through for me earlier.

I dropped the shopping onto the back seat of my car, next to Freya's car seat, which she would have to use until she was eleven (or one hundred and forty centimetres as the manual said, whichever came first). As she was only five I had a long time to wait. The sooner we got rid of that car seat the better. I drove as fast as I could through the busy afternoon town, which was only letting me do about ten miles per hour. Half the world appeared to be out running errands or trying to get from one place to another. There seemed to be quite a few parents like me around, dashing across roads and hurrying back to big tank-like SUVs on the last push to get things done before the school run.

I couldn't risk being late. Fifteen minutes or so after the designated pick up time, the school starts making phone calls, and inevitably Steph's mobile is the first on the list. Not only would there be the embarrassment of not being there on time to collect your child, who was supposed to be (and was) the most precious thing in your world, but then you had to deal with the fallout from the child itself, crying because she was the last one to be picked up after having suffered the mounting drama of watching the door to the classroom open twenty-five times, only to see that it wasn't them being collected. And if Steph got a call from the school while she was in Geneva on this conference I'd seriously be in the shit.

It didn't go as far as a phone call, which was a relief. The worst of it was a grim look from Mrs Hill. Freya ran to me when I appeared at the door to her classroom. She gave me a huge hug around my legs which made my heart want to escape my chest. When she released me, I walked over to her tiny table and loaded myself up with her lunchbox, coat, a painting of a summer scene and her cardigan. I consoled myself with the fact there was one other boy in the classroom waiting to be collected.

I clipped Freya into her car seat, checked the straps and clips, then double-checked. Then triple-checked, dammit. Freya seemed preoccupied with singing but every time I put her into her car seat I'd wait for her to say something. Not this time. One day she would. I'd just have to hope there was no one else in the car when she did.

As I pulled out of the school car park she came out with, 'Is it swimming tonight Daddy?'

And suddenly my face drained of blood. Was it tonight? I couldn't remember. Would I need to text Steph and look incompetent? No, no... it was Thursday. It was definitely Thursday. 'Not tonight my love. Tonight, it's just Freya and Daddy time. I've got us lasagne and garlic bread.'

'Yesss!'

'And ice cream too,' I said. I'd pulled up to a red light, so I raised my head, so I could catch a glimpse of her in the rear-view mirror.

'Monty chocolat?'

She always tried to say it in French after Steph had taken her to Geneva once. 'Yes, mint choc chip.'

We parked up outside my building. When we got into the flat I swapped my suit for another pair of shorts and a t-shirt. Freya wanted to stay in her school clothes. We played Pop-Up Pirates on the coffee table. There was something about that game that made her laugh so fully that I couldn't help but laugh too and my eyes would fill up with real tears. I'd never let her see me have that reaction, but I also didn't think it would matter if she did.

Then we built stuff with Lego Duplo. She was too young for

the normal Lego, but she was good with the bigger bricks. We made the tallest tower we could and when it fell down it took us ages to find all the pieces as they'd gone under the sofa and the TV cabinet.

We ate dinner at six and by seven I had her in the bath. And all this time my mind was thinking about the C Type batteries. About the radio. About the frequency.

I washed her hair with Unicorn Shampoo, chased her round the flat as she ran off wet with a towel round her, singing some pop song at the top of her voice (pitch perfect I was staggered to discover) and laughing. I found the towel crumpled in the hall and her jumping up and down on her bed.

'Come on let's get your hair dry.'

Steph had put Freya's Gruffalo Trunki case in her room. For a moment I wondered if Steph might have snooped around the flat a bit when she had it to herself earlier. Looked in the fridge to see if I was eating properly. Checked the laundry basket to see if I was keeping on top of the washing. I opened the Trunki and retrieved Freya's pyjamas, the tangle teaser for her hair, her Moana toothbrush and toothpaste from her washbag. I hung up her school uniform. Putting her pyjamas on was like trying to put a set of Christmas lights back into the box, made less easy by her slightly damp skin. Three times in a row I got both of her legs down one trouser leg. All the time she was yelling 'I'm colllldddd!'

'But it's the hottest week of the year!'

I put the hair drier on her hair and put it in a bobble while she wrestled with her Kyoot Spighdaz Blind Bag wrapper. I opened the toy for her, read her three stories and refused a fourth despite her pleading. I tucked her into bed with Jeremy the pink rabbit, and Miss Wincy, the blue toy she had now "collected", and kissed her goodnight. It was still very light outside, so I put a suction cup blackout blind on the window to try to convince her it was night time.

It was eight o'clock.

I waited and looked at my phone in the kitchen long enough to be satisfied that she might be asleep. Then I checked on her.

Sometimes she would still be awake, then she'd get up and start pinballing round the flat, and I'd have to start all over again, but this time I was lucky. She was fast asleep with one leg thrust out the side of the bed. I levered it back in. She mumbled something unintelligible and rolled over.

◆ ◆ ◆

The radio.

In the lounge, at the coffee table, I gave the contacts in the battery compartment a bit of a wipe with a piece of kitchen roll to remove the last of the oxidisation, then I fitted two new C Types into the trench. When I switched on the radio I was presented with BBC Radio Two at full volume. Wincing, I turned the sound down, waited a few moments to satisfy myself I hadn't woken my daughter, then switched the band over to SW and twisted the knob to move up through the frequencies. On the sticky note copied from the jigsaw, still stuck to the table, I had written the frequency number 15733khz.

Lots of hissing and static. Then I reached 15733khz and heard squelchy, echoey white noise. Nothing of any significance. I started to twist the knob more to move away and back and heard what sounded like African music; distant, bubbling and fizzing on the airwaves. Suddenly there was a world out there, across the continents, talking to each other, existing outside of the small confines of Chalkweald. It made me feel connected in a new way, like the Internet used to when I first discovered it. I went the other way, back through the African music, and beyond 15733khz going downwards. A woman speaking quickly in French. I think she was talking about football. I returned to 15733khz. Again, just squelchy, echoey noise.

Later I was pottering in the kitchen, tidying up dinner, it was just before ten o'clock. I had left the radio on, hissing static quietly in the lounge. The last of the warm light was almost gone from the still evening. Suddenly the white noise stopped, and the radio started talking. An older male voice speaking slowly and deliberately in Received English with no emotion as if reading wartime news.

On Southern green 'neath bluest heaven,
We met once between rhododendron and birch,
But those scents were not so striking when our embrace,
Connected again between land and sky,
So divine a gift I cannot recreate,
On this field or another,
Because pure yearning disappears,
With the clouding of an ageing province.

Then after a short pause.

Four-seven-five-three.
Six-three-one-nine.
Two-five-nine-seven.

Listening I slowly put the tea-towel on the kitchen worktop, my drying up unfinished, and took a few steps towards the door to the lounge.

Eight-two-eight-four.
One-four-seven-eight.

I picked up the pad of sticky notes and a pen from the kitchen worktop and went through to sit on the sofa. I started writing down the numbers. Is this what David Wenlock, my jigsaw sender, wanted me to hear?

When I'd written down about fifty or so sets of numbers, tacking the top of each note to the bottom of the previous one, I saw movement at the corner of my eye.

I looked up and saw Freya standing at the door, rubbing her eyes, holding Jeremy.

The numbers carried on while I picked her up and carried her back to bed, trying to hurry, but trying not to make it look to Freya like I was hurrying. She said something that sounded a bit like "muddle", and then half laughed and half giggled in a way that I'd not heard her do before. More guttural than I was used to. As I lay her down in her bed she stared at me and didn't seem to be focusing on me. And that was when I realised that she wasn't really awake. But not really asleep either. Halfway between.

She rolled over and that was the end of it.

When I got back to the lounge the radio had stopped giving out numbers. It was ten thirty-five. I picked up my phone and started to enter the numbers I'd written on the sticky notes into a Notes Document. Having them on sticky notes didn't seem to be the wisest way to record them. I had written down about one hundred sets of four numbers, but I reckon there had been approximately a hundred and fifty sets read out in total. I'd missed a whole section of them while I was putting Freya back to bed. Once I'd transferred the numbers I'd written over to my phone notes I put the date above them as a heading. If these numbers were read out at ten o'clock every night I might want to know which day was which.

In search of some sort of validation I wanted to look at the completed jigsaw again, but I'd collapsed it, hadn't I? I wanted to look at the photo I'd taken, but I'd deleted it, hadn't I? I'd copied down the frequency correctly. And there it was. There was no denying what had happened here. The intention was clear.

Who are you, David Wenlock? And what are you trying to tell me?

I switched the light off in the kitchen and the lounge, checked the front door was locked and looked in on Freya. Then I went into my bedroom. Outside the window in the still heat it was dark now. I could hear distant cars on the Chalkweald bypass and an owl having a one-way conversation with the night.

I switched off the light in the bedroom, intending to get undressed by the light of the streetlight coming through the window. I went to partially close the curtains and froze mid-pull when I saw a man standing out there, across the road, just to the left of where the oak foliage obscured the opposite pavement. I couldn't make out any of his features because he was out of the catchment of the nearest streetlamp, but I could see that he was looking directly at my building. Hands by his sides. Not moving. Whether he thought he couldn't be seen I don't know. But I could damn well see him.

I found myself uttering. 'What the hell...?'

Was it David Wenlock? This elusive Facebooker sent me the jigsaw so he knew where I lived.

My house keys were in the kitchen, so I picked them up quickly, put on some slip-on shoes over my bare feet and went outside and down the steps. It didn't occur to me that the man might be a danger. As I reached the end of the walkway beside the buildings I saw that he had started to move quickly away.

I called out across the road. 'Can I help you?'

The man stopped and turned. He lifted his hand to shade the streetlight from his eyes, He said, 'Is that you Chris?'

I recognised his voice. 'Eamonn?'

There had been no cars along the road. He waited while I crossed by my car, skirted around the grass triangle and approached him. He was wearing an army surplus green jacket, an army green t-shirt and jeans.

'Hi mate,' I said, trying to sound anything but suspicious. 'Everything ok?'

'Yeah, the dog's taking me for a walk again. We've been up to Tilmere Woods. He likes it up there.'

'Where's the dog?' I said.

'Oh,' he uttered a small laugh. 'Probably gone off to find some bush to shit in. He catches up eventually.'

I tried to laugh with him. I was sure I sounded fake. And was pretty sure Eamonn knew me well enough to know when

I'm laughing with zero conviction. But I hoped he didn't suss me. Because wasn't that exactly what he'd said to the onesie lady two nights ago? Something about the dog shitting in a bush and catching up. He must've thought that line was new on me. That was all very well, but I still hadn't seen the dog.

In the darkness of one of Malcom Renfield's upper windows I thought I saw a curtain fall back into place. There's not normally so much activity in this quiet road, anything of note tends to get at least one curtain-twitcher. Two nights ago, I was that curtain twitcher. It brought me out here. This was getting to be a habit.... And then it hit me.

The numbers! Yesterday the police officer's wife had said in the bread aisle that Malcom Renfield had been listening to numbers on his radio. With that massive antenna on his roof he had to be into all this stuff. The distraction was momentary, but then Eamonn spoke.

'Anyway, good to see you mate'. He started to move to walk away along Chalkweald Avenue.

I called after him, trying to sound like none of this was as weird as hell. "Oh, by the way I spoke to Valerie about the entrance path change and she was up for it. She's taking it up the chain and she thought it was a cracking idea. Once I knew how well it had been received I made sure you got the credit for it.'

After a moment, Eamonn said, 'Thanks Chris I really appreciate it. It's nice to be recognised when you put good ideas forward, so that's really good to hear.'

'No problem,' I managed a smile and pointed in the direction he had started to walk, 'Now go find that pooch!'

I walked back across Wellowteme Crescent towards my building. I deliberately didn't look back to see whether Eamonn was actually walking away or whether he had stopped again. Part of me didn't *want* to know, because I think if I had seen him stop again, I wouldn't have known how to deal with it.

And still there was no dog.

What are you up to, Eamonn?

Back in the flat I bolted the front door. I don't normally throw the big bolt. Then I crept down the hall to look in on Freya again. A couple of the suction cups on her blackout-blind had come away from the window so I licked them and placed them back. Freya was in the same position as before. I went to get a closer look and to satisfy myself she was still breathing, because when you can't immediately hear it, you go and check. And that instinct wasn't going to go away anytime soon.

Of course, as ever, it was one of those times where she appeared to be holding her breath in Dreamland, and then just as you get close enough she exhales in one big long breath, and you feel foolish for thinking it and creep away.

I propped myself up in bed in the dark with my laptop warming my thighs and Googled the radio frequency "15733khz". The first result that came up referred to a website called TOLWORTH-RELAY.NET which claimed to "Livestream the Tolworth Beacon 24/7"

I wasn't sure what any of that meant but the next website in the search results caught my eye. The heading read...

Numbers Stations. What are they? And who runs them?

I clicked into the page and started to read.

"Gentlemen don't read each other's mail." Henry L Stimpson, US Cypher Bureau.

Ever since the beginning of language, people have been trying to keep information secret. Spies smuggle data in a variety of ingenious ways. Some wrote messages on their shaved heads, and then let their hair grow before travelling abroad. Microfilms were hidden inside timepieces and bars of soap. But during the Cold War, when tensions between the US and the USSR were at their highest, another form of international-range monologue gained prominence. Numbers Stations. With specific Interval Signals, these mysterious radio broadcasts have been given nicknames among the enthusiasts who are fascinated by them. With names such as The Lincolnshire Poacher, Magnetic Fields and The Tolworth Beacon, these radio stations send signals on the shortwave radio band. When directed at the ionosphere, shortwave signals reflect back down to Earth at great distances beyond the horizon, allowing an almost global reach, especially at night. These stations have been broadcasting for decades. Given the cost required to set up and maintain such stations, and the fact that they are unlicensed and therefore illegal, it is assumed that they must be funded and operated by governments. But no government has ever admitted to operating one. The widely accepted theory is that these radio stations would transmit numbers that could only be deciphered in the field by spies with a specific pad which would enable them to decode the numbers back into a message. These messages are unbreakable without the pad, which only the sender and the recipient would own a copy of. And because all a spy would need is a common household radio, this would make them practically undetectable by an enemy. It is also assumed that a Numbers Station may continue broadcasting even when it's not required, as deploying a station only when it's needed might give a clue as to who is operating it.

But it isn't only numbers that haunt the shortwave frequencies. Other stations such as The Pip, Chimes and Gongs, The Squeaky Wheel and The Buzzer issue sinister sounds across the airwaves, for reasons we can only guess at.

I tapped BACK and went into the TOLWORTH-RELAY.NET site. Clearly a page made by one such Numbers Station enthusiast, probably in his bedroom, this black page contained a yellow box with what looked like a long sound file which was being constructed in real-time on the screen, new scribbles of sound coming in from the left, and disappearing off to the right. There was a slider bar at the bottom which you could use to select a time-period for the visible bit of the soundwave, which was currently set to 24 hours. There was also a mute icon and when I tapped it, the mute went off and I could hear the radio station hissing and squelching. Looking at the sound waves it was possible to see from their stepped shape when the speech was happening and when the station was "silent". Looking at the sound waves and the scrolling window, it was possible to listen to any part of the stream going back six years, as far as 2014. There was also a note on the page stating that the station had been broadcasting since 1982.

I scrolled down the page and found a CONTACT ME button. I pressed it, it opened a blank email on my laptop, and typed:

Hello, I need to talk to you about The Tolworth Beacon. Is there a phone number I can call you on?

I read my email a couple of times, wondering whether I should write more. Then I hit SEND. It occurred to me, if only I'd Googled the frequency last night. I could have saved myself the hassle of finding a radio and buying batteries.

I switched off the laptop and put it on the floor, sliding it slightly under the bed so I didn't accidentally step on it if I got up in the night. Then I took a quick peek around the curtains to see if Eamonn had returned. But he was nowhere to be seen.

WEDNESDAY

Freya climbed in bed with me about ten minutes before my phone alarm was due to go off at six. She nuzzled up to me and I kissed her warm head. Freya, little Freya who we could have lost. She was whispering something to herself, a rhyme or something.

It happened back in March. Four months ago. When we could have lost her. I remember it was a clear, crisp, blue day and Steph, Freya and I had driven out to Chalkweald Manor, a National Trust property which had a great adventure park and den-building area for kids. We'd taken the old car. After a few hours of stomping around in the woods, Freya had muddy wellies and I took them off her while I was carrying her back to the car, getting mud on my coat as I did so. I wrestled the boots off with one hand and passed them to Steph, so she could put them on some newspaper in the boot. I fastened Freya into her car seat. At least, I thought I did.

Chalkweald Manor was about six miles away from where we lived on the outskirts of Chalkweald town itself. The quickest way home was to take the bypass to get back to our side of town. It was about three in the afternoon and the temperature outside was half a degree above zero according to the dashboard. There had been some ice about, even the stubborn remnants of snow in some places after a substantial downfall we'd had five days earlier. I was taking it reasonably carefully. Steph had made pulled pork in the slow cooker and had said something earlier about wanting to get back to check it. I can't blame her for any sense of urgency that I might have felt. No, this was all on me.

I remember Steph and I were talking about booking a week away somewhere in the summer. Steph fancied Greece. She'd been before but I never had. We didn't get very far with the conversation.

Just near to Chalkweald Avenue there's a Forestry Commission road that cuts through Tilmere Woods. Unless you were shortcutting to one of the roads around where we lived you wouldn't bother with it as there are better roads to get you elsewhere. I'd taken this shortcut to get us home and was doing less than thirty miles an hour when our car ran onto some black ice. The steering wheel of the car went light in my hands, like it had voluntarily given up trying to control the car, which of course it had, and the back end started to slide out to the right. I couldn't have lost control for more than two seconds and I'd lost a little bit of speed but when the tyres purchased the road again we continued at about twenty-seven miles an hour in the direction of one of Tilmere Wood's many tall and beautiful Scots pines. I swore as I pumped the brake, and although I halved our speed we hit the tree at a fair lick. Staggeringly the airbags didn't deploy, although perhaps they should have, I don't know. Thankfully seat belts stopped us from flying forward. But there was nothing to stop Freya as her seat unleashed her. She squealed as her body launched forward into the back of Steph's seat. She crumpled down into the footwell. It was a terrifying thump sound. She started crying immediately, which believe it or not was some consolation. It's when there's no sound you have to worry, right? Steph had started to shriek through quick shallow pulsing breaths. Calling Freya's name. The definitive sound of deep fear rising from my wife's throat, something I'd never heard before and will never, ever forget. Because I knew what was going through her mind, and it wasn't just Freya. Her family had history with seatbelts. She and I both knew that Freya had come free of her seat, but I had a better angle to look and, in that moment, I didn't care about anything else other than whether our fragile little girl was alright, I didn't even care about Steph's wellbeing. I released my seat belt and twisted round. I felt stiffness in my neck. I could see Freya down there lying on her front, with her head near her car door (but not against it) and her right leg, her shin, resting on the rear part of the central panel between the front seats, her white socked foot pointing at me. I threw open my door and ran around the back of the car to Freya's side. I knew she wasn't against the door, so I opened it quickly and Freya lifted her head, crying crying crying. Her cheeks were shiny with tears, but there were no visible cuts or grazes. I went to grab her, and Steph shouted for me to stop, stop because Freya might have injured herself. And then Steph was out of the car. She came around the door and shoved me to the right, her entire focus on Freya, asking if she was ok, if there was anywhere that hurt, where had she banged herself, both of us undoubtedly thinking her head, her back, her neck, her *neck!* Normally the pines smelled sweet but there was an acid sourness to the world at that moment. Steph was a First Aider at her work and after a minute or so she seemed to be satisfied that there was no serious damage done, so she fished our daughter out of the footwell and gathered her up. Freya wrapped her legs around her mother, still crying but less now, hitching her breath, her head buried into Steph's neck.

And then the questions came. Didn't you fasten her in? Yes, I swear I did, something must have broken like the clips or the straps. Well you can't have done. And then, absurdly, to try and acquit myself I was giving the car seat a once over because now I knew we were all ok the next thing was whose fault it was, and it was obviously mine, unless the seat was fucked. Either the seat was fucked, or I was. I checked the five-point harness, all the clips and sockets. I pulled on each of the belts, but they were all fine, weren't they? Of course they were. All bloody fine. Everything with the seat was just bloody fine. The look that Steph gave me when we both realised there was nothing wrong with the seat. *That look.* That was the moment. It was the moment that started the ball rolling. The moment that led to today. It was the moment that led to Freya and Steph living at Steph's Mum's place. Because how do you get back from that?

The car had a whopping dent in the front, the bonnet was crumpled, but that could be fixed (and it *was* the next day; I told the garage I had been driving alone, and after that we sold it and bought the Corsa). The engine started, and we were still able to drive home. The bigger dilemma was whether we should have taken Freya to hospital. We had a furious whispering row about it in the kitchen twenty minutes later while Freya played with dolls in the lounge as though nothing had happened. Both of us were acutely aware that a visit to the hospital would invite questions and we would have to tell the truth about the car seat not being fastened properly, because as soon as you start lying and the story doesn't fit with what the doctors see then there would be more questions. Questions that, in our frightened paranoid minds would lead to Freya being taken away from us because we were not fit to be her parents and it was all my fault. And Steph didn't want to lose another member of her family because of a car. We'd have visits from social services. And because I had caused this. Because I had inflicted this situation on Steph, on us, she found it impossible to forgive me. Even as little as a day later it was too late to change our minds about the hospital. There was no going back on our decision because there would still be questions. Harder questions. Why didn't we bring her in yesterday? So, you'd have to compound the lie with another lie. And what would they ask Freya in private? What would she tell them?

Our decision, while mutual, festered and grew mouldy, the effluent of it polluting deep marital waters.

In the end I was surprised that she would be the one to leave, and undermine her own chances of domestic bliss, the cornerstone of her sanity.

I showered while Freya watched the birthdays on Cbeebies. Then we got dressed, me in my work suit, which required the additional activity of ironing a shirt, Freya in her school uniform. I texted Clem from the breakfast table while watching Freya eat chocolate croissants and the dusty dregs of a Shreddies packet which had been in the cupboard for months. *Going to be a bit late. Need to drop Freya at school.*

There was another reason too. I wanted to talk to Malcolm Renfield about the radio broadcast he'd been listening to when that policewoman was in there, the one the tall officer's wife gossiped about to her friend in the supermarket. I'd avoided going to Malcolm earlier, but that was before I heard the broadcast.

Clem texted back. *OK see you later.*

I dropped Freya at school, making a point of being first through the door so Mrs Hill would take notice, although she was talking to her assistant when we arrived and didn't pay any attention to the order the pupils were arriving in.

I drove back to Wellowteme Crescent, parked outside my building and crossed the road to number twenty-two, Malcolm Renfield's detached house. As I walked over there I noticed that his white Porsche Cayenne, the car he had retrieved his Mag-Lite from the other night, wasn't in the drive.

I rang the doorbell anyway, chimes echoing inside, and as I expected there was no answer. I stepped back from the door, looked right and saw that the living room curtains were open, and it didn't look like there was any furniture in there. I stepped behind a rosebush that was under the window, catching my suit jacket on its thorny stalks, and peeked around the edge of the living room window. Sure enough, the place was totally empty right down to the sandy coloured carpets, there was not an item of furniture in that room, and there were faded sections of the wall where pictures had been taken down.

Walking back along the drive I looked up at the upstairs windows to see if there was any activity, and I noticed that the big antenna was gone from the roof. It was dark last night so I hadn't noticed whether the antenna was there when I was talking to Eamonn outside the house, but it was definitely there in the early hours of Monday when we'd congregated out here after the burglary, I mean, after the attempted burglary. I saw it silhouetted by the moon.

Ok so what the hell was going on? Two days ago, Malcolm Renfield was living here. Then after an attempted burglary which seemed to bring out the vigilante in him, rather than the coward, he moves out and takes his roof antenna with him. Didn't I see him twitching at the curtains last night? Perhaps I was mistaken. I know I hadn't been here all the time but when the hell did he move out? Well, it can only have been during the day on Monday or Tuesday while I was at work.

And separately, Eamonn had been acting strangely. I knew I wasn't mistaken when I saw him out of my window. He was standing there. He wasn't walking. He was watching my building. He wasn't walking a dog. There was no dog. There is no dog. It wasn't off shitting in a bush on two separate nights, because it didn't exist. He said he was walking this dog but instead he was walking alone. If there was no dog, then why had he come out to stare at my building?

◆ ◆ ◆

When I got to the deliveries entrance I saw Max walking quickly across the floor towards me.

'Eamonn hasn't turned up for work,' he said. I've tried to call his phone but it's just going to voicemail.'

I said, 'I'll try him.'

And I did. But all I got was 'Hi this is Eamonn. Leave a message.'

Shaking my head at Max I said. 'Hi Eamonn, Chris here. Just checking everything's okay as you've not turned up this morning. Give me a call when you get this. Ok. Bye.'

By eleven o'clock I was beginning to worry. Lateness was not in Eamonn's repertoire. Perhaps punctuality had been drilled into him in the forces. On my computer I double-checked the global rota spreadsheet to ensure he didn't have annual leave booked. He didn't. Besides, I think he said "See you tomorrow" last night. Or had he?

I popped into Clem's office, jangling my car keys between my fingers.

One of the cleaners was in there, a short young girl with severe acne called Cerys. She and Clem were in mid conversation about a customer who had somehow managed to drop a whole load of his shopping, which he'd been trying to carry without a basket.

'He was in the fruit section,' Cerys said. 'And he dropped everything, and stuff rolled under the shelving racks.'

'Anything perishable?' said Clem.

'He said not. I had a look under there and I saw a shampoo bottle and a deodorant, and some stuff from the kitchenware aisle. A kitchen knife and a pack of cutlery. I got most of it out, but I reckon we'll have to have the racks out the way to get it all.'

Clem had been my deputy for about eight months. He had quite the hipster look going on. He was twenty-three, had a full head of well-tended brown hair and a U-shaped beard that was so immaculately crafted that it looked like it required him to set his alarm for half an hour earlier in the mornings than he would if he didn't have it.

Clem said, 'Thanks for letting me know Cerys. Much appreciated. We'll sort it out.'

Cerys left the office.

I said, 'I'm going to take a drive up to Eamonn's flat.'

Clem turned in his chair to his computer screen. 'Shall we have a look at the CCTV?'

'For what?'

'For the epic fail in the fruit aisle.'

A small laugh escaped me. 'Ok.'

I went around the side of Clem's desk so that we could both look at his computer monitor. I always marvelled at how tidy he kept his desk. Keyboard, mouse, USB fan and square mug coaster. All geometrically aligned.

Clem pulled up the CCTV software, selected the image for the fruit section and wound the feed back half an hour. He then played it at four-times speed until a blonde-haired man with a thin face walked onto the screen, laden down with a bunch of items and proceeded to accidentally spill all of them onto the floor. A yogurt pot exploded by his feet and a load of other bits skidded across the floor in all directions, some going under the racks holding the bananas and melons.

Clem laughed, 'What an idiot! Doesn't he realise we have trolleys and baskets for a reason!'

Seconds later on the video, Cerys is there helping the man. She clears up the yogurt with a mop and she says something to him, reassuring him by the looks of it. He picks up a couple of items and then walks off. Cerys remains and is trying to fish out the items that have skidded under the shelving. After some time, she stands up holding some of them.

Clem said. 'I'll get the racks moved later and we'll pick up whatever else was dropped.'

'I need to get over to Eamonn's,' I said.

Clem closed the CCTV application. 'I would come with you but one of us needs to be here.'

'I won't be long.'

'Depends what you find,' he said. 'Hope he's ok.'

I went out to my Corsa and drove over to Eamonn's. He lived fifteen minutes away on the eighteenth floor of a block of flats called Meander's Reach. It was one of the buildings that overlooked a wide section of the Malbrook, the river that weaved through Chalkweald and curved widely around a large green space where these buildings were situated. The green space boasted a substantial play park that Steph and I had brought Freya to on many occasions.

There was a small car-park for residents at the foot of Meander's Reach, close to the entrance to the park where an ice-cream van chugged away. I knew which space Eamonn normally used. But his blue Peugeot was nowhere to be seen. I got out and walked across the hot tarmac to the ground floor entrance. I buzzed his intercom. No reply. I waited a few minutes and tailgated a young mother with a pram and got into the lift to his floor.

I knocked on his door (number 46) but still there was no answer. I checked my phone to see if he'd replied to my messages. He hadn't. I rang his landline, and I could hear it ringing inside. There was no answer, so I hung up.

My phone buzzed. Ah, here we go.

But it wasn't Eamonn, it was Steph. *Just landed at Gatwick. Freya ok?*

I tapped out a reply. *Yes, all good. She's safely dropped at school.*

'And I'm ok too thanks for asking,' I heard myself mutter.

Steph's response was. *I'll pick up her things this afternoon.*

I replied, *Her Trunki is all packed in her room.*

And so, this game of dodging each other continued. She could come over in the evening and collect it, but that would involve us having a "conversation". I'd take her and Freya back in an instant, but it was Steph's call. It had now been two and a half weeks since we'd had the latest row. After which she and our daughter moved out.

I drove back to Hollyways. Part of me wanted to call the police about Eamonn. Part of me thought I was being paranoid. But in the light of his absence from work this morning I was more convinced that his behaviour last night was odd.

I went to my desk drawer and retrieved the master key to the staff lockers. I called Clem's phone and asked him if he would pop into my office.

'How did you get on?' he asked.

'There's no sign of him at home and he's not answering his mobile or landline,' I held up the locker master key. 'I don't know about you but I'm getting worried, so I want to have a look in his locker to see if there's any indication as to what's happened to him.'

'We'll do it together,' he said, and that seemed like the best idea.

The row of lockers was in our large staff room. A couple of the cleaners were at a table on the other side of the room, drinking paper coffee, looking at something together on one of their phones.

Clem watched as I opened Eamonn's locker.

Eamonn's picture was staring at us from the inside door, grinning, hot in the desert, with his rocket propelled grenade launcher. Bundled inside the small space were a black hoodie, a white t-shirt and a pair of dirty white trainers that gave the whole locker a bit of a cheesy whiff. And a can of deodorant. Underneath the trainers was a book. I took it out in case there were any bits of paper in it. Phone numbers or something. It was a thin novel called "The Gathering Hand" by Emma Hicksmeyer. Not a book I'd ever heard of. It looked well thumbed, especially the first half. On the cover was a watercolour painting of a man in farmer's clothes standing on a hill beside a lone tree, looking into the distance, and at the top, next to the title, someone had written SPARE COPY in blue biro.

I flicked through the pages but there were no bits of paper or anything, just a load of densely scribbled text on the inside of the front cover. It was Eamonn's handwriting.

OC4316
15733 kHz Suppressed Lower Sideband
The Singularity!
Joshua Daly. Wow!!
22 Wellowteme Crescent.
Malcolm Renfield = David Wenlock! REALLY???
Haleswade Leap NT CP. North Three miles. Ord surv no?

'What's all that?' said Clem, partly looking at what I was reading, but also reluctant to, as though it was some sort of breach of Eamonn's privacy and therefore above his pay-grade.

'There's nothing here is there?' I said, closing the book, aware that there were things in that book that I needed more time to read and digest.

'Shall we call the police?' said Clem, 'Report him missing? I don't think anyone else is going to.'

I shook my head. 'Shall we give it a little longer? But if we haven't heard anything by mid-afternoon then let's think about it.'

'I wonder if there's a problem with the dog he's been looking after,' Clem said.

'He told you about the dog?'

'Yeah he was looking after one for a friend.'

There is no dog.

With Clem there I couldn't just take the book, despite my need to re-read and digest the things Eamonn had written, so I placed it back in the locker. I didn't want Clem to have any sense that I knew more than I was letting on. I would have to come back later to get it. What was alarming was that Eamonn had written down the name David Wenlock, my Facebook jigsaw sender. Had he caught sight of the message correspondence I had with Mike the Vault yesterday? When Mike was asking me to contact him on WhatsApp about the disappearance of David Wenlock, Eamonn had been talking to me at the time and I had a vague sense he had been trying to read my screen.

Did he pick the name up from my screen, or did he already know who David Wenlock was? No, because I didn't know David Wenlock was David Wenlock until I'd had the WhatsApp call with Mike the Vault, and that was later. In other words, I was pretty sure there was no reference to David Wenlock on my phone screen when Eamonn was trying to look at it.

And what about Eamonn's statement in the front page of the book, that David Wenlock was Malcolm Renfield? What did that mean?

By three-pm when there was still no sign of Eamonn, Clem popped his head round the door of my office.

'What do you want to do?' he said.

I let out a weary sigh. 'I've been mithering him to put next of kin data into the HR system, but I know he hasn't.'

Clem came forward and sat on the chair opposite me. 'What about this Joshua Daly? Might it be worth trying to contact him?'

'The name in the book?' I shook my head. 'That's... That's not a real person.'

But, I thought, *why write "Joshua Daly! WOW!!"?*

'How do you know he's not real?' Clem added.

Because it's the name he's going to give to his son. Who doesn't exist. His son who doesn't exist yet.

I had to break away from the questioning. 'I'm going to nip up to his place again. See if there's any sign of him. Let's give him till tomorrow. Then we'll report it.'

Clem stood up. 'If there's anything you need let me know. I do hope he hasn't come to any harm.'

My phone pinged. Clem went back to his office.

The text was from Steph. *Bag collected, thanks.*

A covert way of telling me she'd been and gone and was out the way, so I could go home without bumping into her.

I heard Clem's phone ring.

I was about to reply to Steph, but instead I put my phone back in my pocket.

Clem answered his phone and I took the opportunity to head back down to the staff room to retrieve "The Gathering Hand" from Eamonn's locker. I took it straight out to my car, got in and put it in the glove compartment. As I was putting my seatbelt on my phone pinged. I took it out of my trouser pocket and saw I had an email reply from someone called Shaun. I opened the email.

Hi there, happy to help you with whatever you want to know. As you can tell from my website, Numbers Stations are a fascination of mine (and lots of other people too). I'm around for the next few hours if you wanna WhatsApp me. Have a good day, Shaun.

The car had been sitting in still July heat for the last few hours. The dashboard told me it was twenty-six degrees. The steering wheel was hot where it had sat in the direct sun. I blasted the air-conditioning as I drove the same route out to Eamonn's place. I was starting to get a headache. Probably dehydration in this heat. I'd not drunk enough water today.

Eamonn's Peugeot still wasn't in the car park at Meander's Reach when I got there so I didn't bother to go into the building. I rang his phone and got his voicemail again.

'Eamonn it's Chris. We're all getting a bit worried about you now mate, to the point where I've been thinking about digging out your next of kin info from your HR record. But, wait, hang on, you didn't email it in the end, did you? So, I'm all at sea trying to work out where you are. I'm ok to chalk today up as Emergency Leave but I need to hear from you. Where are you? Call me back as soon as you can.'

I ended the call and exhaled loudly in the silence of the car. Looking out the window I could see three young boys kicking a football against a garage door at the edge of the car park. The clanging sound was making my headache worse.

I went home, got changed into shorts and a t-shirt. I threw open all the windows, pulled a beer out of the fridge and sat on the sofa with my phone. Shaun answered my WhatsApp video call almost immediately.

'How's it going?' He was American, his receding brown hair had a small tuft at the front, He had two chins and was a little sweaty, with a round face, or was it just a quirk of phone camera lenses? He looked like he was sitting in some sort of study with shelves of books behind him.

'I'm good thanks. And thank you for making yourself available for a chat.'

'No problem. What do you want to know about Numbers Stations?'

I gave a small laugh. 'All of it. I know what Numbers Stations are. I've listened to the Tolworth Beacon. I was listening to it last night.'

'Damn creepy isn't it? They all are. You hear these numbers being beamed out across the airways, in between the static and the white noise. It's like you're listening to the secrets of the Earth. A one directional phone call to God-knows-who, and God-knows-where. And you know you can't decipher them without a one-time-pad.'

I took a gulp of beer. 'What's a one-time-pad?'

'Is it hot there? I heard you guys were having a heatwave.'

'Yeah, it's a rare treat. Most of the time it's cold and rainy.'

'Well I guess you're lucky then. Anyways. Ok, so say you're a spy and you have a small book filled with sheets of paper, each one containing a load of numbers. Now, the numbers on the pad mean nothing by themselves. But the only other person who has the same pad of numbers is the broadcaster. Say the first number on your pad is, like, the number three. The broadcast voice gives a number, and you add the two of them together to get a new number, then you match it with the alphabet to get your letter, and you start writing the letters down to make words. So, a three shown on your pad, plus, say, a seven read out on the broadcast would equal ten, which would give you the letter J. Are you with me?'

'Yes, so far.'

'But because you or I don't have the one-time-pad, it's impossible for us to decode the message just from the numbers being read out by the Station. It's completely uncrackable without the other half of the equation. After decoding the message, the spy can just tear the page out, and I dunno, eat it, flush it, burn it, to destroy any evidence. Whatever. But sometimes you don't need a pad, just an agreed text, like a textbook or something. You just both got to have the same copy, so that you can...'

Shivers launched up my back. Nerves crawled on my scalp. I had to ask. 'So... so how does it work with a book?'

'Well, ok, so if both the broadcaster and the, you know, "spy", both have a copy of the same book, then the broadcaster just needs to read out a set of numbers that correspond with a place in the book. You get something like... page, paragraph or line, word, letter. Something like that. The numbers come in blocks that then allow the spy to decode the letters by locating them in the book. The problem is, unless you know what the book is, the code is just as uncrackable as it is without the one-time-pad.'

'Fascinating stuff,' I said, desperate to go and get Eamonn's book which I'd left in the glove compartment of the Corsa.

Shaun continued. 'But there are other types of broadcast stations. All just as eerie to listen to. You've got The Pip, the Squeaky Wheel. Take UVB-76 for example, also called The Buzzer. Well the Buzzer doesn't even transmit numbers. Just a buzzing sound every two seconds or so. It's been doing so twenty-four hours a day since, like, 1982. Once or twice some singing in the background could be heard, which led us all to believe that the Buzzer was being played through a microphone, in a room, rather than being a direct feed from a sound source. That one has been triangulated to a small radio tower on the Russian border with Estonia. Only the Russian government would have the resources to set up and run something like that?'

'But why? What does a repeating buzzing sound do?'

'The thinking is that it's either there to keep a frequency available to make it unattractive to other potential broadcasters, by clogging it with sound. Or, more worryingly, it's a dead man's switch, where, you know, if anything causes UVB-76 to stop broadcasting, then it would trigger a nuclear retaliation offensive. Mutually Assured Destruction they call it, on the basis that The Buzzer would only stop broadcasting if it had been taken out by an attack. Some say the Russians have radars at Chernobyl that detect changes in the ionosphere which can tell if missiles have been launched from the United States. With all the Cold War stuff it's hard, well, impossible to know what's true, and what these governments were up to, and still are. There are all sorts of conspiracy theories out there. But take away all the theories and you're still left with those radio stations. They're still there, they fascinate us, and we like listening.'

'What about the Tolworth Beacon?'

'The Tolworth Beacon is like the Lincolnshire Poacher, which is a Numbers Station they triangulated as coming originally from Bletchley Park in the UK and then from Cyprus and was thought to be operated by the British Secret Intelligence Service, that uses the first few bars of an old folk tune as its Interval Signal, to verify to the listener that they are listening to the correct Station, you know, before they start transcribing numbers and trying to decode them. The Tolworth Beacon has been triangulated to somewhere in Oxfordshire in the UK. You can get radio direction-finding facilities for the high frequency bands, which provide a line of transmission to locate the mast site. Only the hardcore enthusiasts are into all that stuff. That poem you hear at the start? It uses a poem by Edmund Tolworth. You know, the one that starts "On Southern green 'neath bluest heaven." He was some English poet from the 1700's. We researched it and the poem is called "Thy Conferment of a Downland Summer", written in something like 1805. It doesn't really matter what the Interval Signal is, a tune or a poem. The fact is that spies then know that the numbers they are receiving are intended for them, to be decoded with the pad that they have in their possession. The Tolworth Beacon broadcasts at three-pm Mountain Standard Time which is where I am in Denver. So that's like, nine or ten-pm where you are in England.'

'It broadcasts at ten-pm here.'

'So, I take the live stream from the radio broadcast and relay it onto the Internet at a delay of about fifteen seconds, which is how long it takes for my home server to run a conversion from the analogue broadcast to the digital soundwave. So, what you hear on my website is like fifteen seconds behind the live radio broadcast. But it's a constant stream. I've been streaming the broadcasts for six years. All the daily messages appear to be the same length, read out over a thirty-minute period. Same as the Lincolnshire Poacher. The assumption is that there may be some irrelevant material in the message, but the broadcasts are kept at the same length to mask the size of the message, and subsequently the level of spy activity being carried out.'

'But isn't a Beacon something that's designed to be seen? Not something spies use.'

'You're right of course. And the Tolworth Beacon is not what it's *really* called. To the people operating it, whoever the hell they are, it will probably have some alpha-numeric designation. But we don't know what that name is, so we just call it The Tolworth Beacon.'

'Who's "we"?'

'A group of enthusiastic listeners who are obsessed with Numbers Stations. We're a radio cryptography group that records, stores and archives broadcasts from Numbers Stations.'

I had all I needed from Shaun. I thanked him for his time, and I was surprised that at no point did he ask me why I was so interested in all this stuff. Maybe he got contacted a lot. He obviously enjoyed talking about The Tolworth Beacon and Numbers Stations and all the other crazy stuff he mentioned.

How strange it was that something so obviously *there*, a radio broadcast that anyone could listen to, was also a carrier of such secrets.

With my copy of 'The Gathering Hand" by Emma Hicksmeyer, retrieved from the car, now on my dining room table, alongside my small painting radio, and my laptop. I sat down and prepared to type out the numbers from this evening's broadcast.

At ten o'clock it started. "Thy Conferment of a Downland Summer". Emerging through the static, which parted like dawn fog burned off by the sun. The male voice spoke.

On Southern green 'neath bluest heaven,
We met once between rhododendron and birch,
But those scents were not so striking when our embrace,
Connected again between land and sky,
So divine a gift I cannot recreate,
On this field or another,
Because pure yearning disappears,
With the clouding of an ageing province.

Then after a pause.

Six-three-nine-one.
Four-five-two-eight

And that was how I spent the next thirty minutes. Tirelessly typing in all the numbers. It had to be done that way when you think about it. A two-step process. Get all the numbers down, and then begin the painstaking process of referencing each number against the book, turning it into a letter.

At ten thirty when the broadcast stopped, I began the work of referencing each number against the "The Gathering Hand" to get my letters. At one point I missed a number and gobbledygook started coming out, so I had to go back almost to the beginning where it stopped making sense and pick up from there. It took me until two in the morning to decode the two-hundred and fifty letters, curated from one-thousand numbers read out, where each set of four in the broadcast resolved to one letter in the book.

OC4316CONFIRMTHATENTRANCEPATHWAYHASBEENLENGTHEN
EDTHISISFINALINSTRUCTIONNOFURTHEROUTCOMECALIBRATIO
NCURRENTLYREQUIREDSTOPOC2341AMAZONACTIVISTSINSITU
AWAITINGCONVOYARRIVALINSTRUCTIONISTOREMAININPOSITI
ONSTOPXGMFYBRNTHFTRDTGIFODNCBYERJFKKDBHFRDUBLUSY
RCVIUJ.

Towards the end, I thought my decoding method had gone awry, but then I recalled how Shaun had referred to extra irrelevant characters in the regular thirty-minute broadcasts to mask the size of the actual message, so as not to give away an increased level of communication activity.

It also occurred to me how clever the overall mechanism was. Anyone eavesdropping on the broadcast with the intention of deciphering it by looking for number patterns that might indicate a repeated word like "THE" would be disappointed. The example within these coded messages was the word "STOP". A repeated word, but not from repeated numbers.

I didn't know much about it, but I saw a documentary once about Alan Turing and his team of codebreakers at Bletchley Park who decoded the Enigma machine messages sent by the Germans in the Second World War. The presence of repeated phrases, such as the names of specific U-Boats, and mention of the weather forecast, were guaranteed and could therefore be relied upon to appear multiple times in certain parts of the message. This element, in combination with other rules and limitations that governed the way the Enigma machine operated, gave Turing's team a framework within which to work. Even then, due to the variance of the dial settings on the Enigma machine, work had to start afresh each time a new message was received.

As I transcribed the letters it became more evident how, with The Tolworth Beacon broadcasts, things were different. Unlike Enigma there were no dial settings to work with. Every iteration of the same word could be spelled out using different number references to other instances of the same letter but elsewhere in the book. The book was essentially random, with no specific rules governing how the letters should be chosen. The letter "D" on one page was just the same as the letter "D" on another page but could be referenced by a completely different number sequence in the spoken broadcast, even within the same message. This enabled the messages to be transferred completely securely to anyone with access to the right decoding book, and, conversely, it couldn't be deciphered by anyone who didn't have access to the book. As Shaun said, it would be uncrackable.

Darkness had crept around me with the waning light. In my concentration I hadn't switched on any lights in the flat. Reading through what I had written I realised that Eamonn had already managed what was being asked of him on this occasion. I recalled he used that word, *Calibrate*, in an odd manner in the early hours of Monday morning. Who he was meant to report back to I had no idea. Perhaps that was where he had gone off to. To deliver a report. There had been a reference to a location in the front cover of 'The Gathering Hand'. Returning to the book I re-read what he had written there.

Haleswade Leap NT CP. North Three miles. Ord surv no?

Had he triangulated the location of The Tolworth Beacon transmissions? Or was this just a covert place to deliver a report, based on something he had received in an older message? Perhaps he had been given that information when he was recruited?

But what sent the most substantial shiver through me, causing me to stand up and turn on some lights to banish the dark corners of the flat, was that if Eamonn had been instructed earlier in the week to try to change the length of the supermarket pathway, and was now being asked to confirm it, *why had he been asked in the first place*?

That discussion he and I had on the shop floor just two days ago. He had couched it in terms of ensuring more people could get into the supermarket to see the unveiling of the plaque by the Duchess on Saturday. What on Earth was a covert Numbers Station doing broadcasting instructions about changing the arrangements of a Royal Visit?

Referring back to Eamonn's inside cover notes in "The Gathering Hand", I had no idea where Haleswade Leap was. There was no way I was going to get there tomorrow, what with the Royalty Protection visit. If I was going to go up there at all, it would have to be Friday. But it *did* have to be before Saturday.

It was late, and I was too tired to do anything more about it now. I wanted to listen to some earlier broadcasts via the TOLWORTH-RELAY.NET website, but the adrenaline of discovery was draining from my system and now sleep was trying to take over.

I undressed and took myself to bed. My thoughts still turning over the possibilities. Thoughts of government communications traversing the airwaves, unbeknownst to almost everyone. How had Eamonn become involved in all of this?

THURSDAY

While I was eating croissants and drinking coffee for breakfast I looked up Haleswade Leap on the Internet. It was a wide escarpment about seventy-five miles north-east of Chalkweald, beyond Oxford. A spot for walks with a nice view over the surrounding countryside on one side and a quarry on the other side, but little else. On Google Maps it said that Haleswade Leap National Trust car-park was less than a two-hour drive from Wellowteme Crescent.

On the way to work I parked in a thirty-minute parking zone on the high street and nipped into Chalkweald Books to purchase two items, but I came away with three.

The first item was a copy of "The Gathering Hand". I needed my own copy so that I could return Eamonn's to his locker. When I found it in the fiction section I compared the two copies to ensure that the page delineations were the same. They were.

The second item was an Ordnance Survey map of the Haleswade Leap area. Google Maps didn't really show much detail and when I switched it to satellite mode I couldn't see any sign of a transmitter three miles north of the National Trust Car Park, assuming I was looking in the right place.

The third item occurred to me while I was in Chalkweald Books. I scoured the biography section for anything about Edmund Tolworth. Despite what Shaun had said about the poem in the Interval Signal being irrelevant, I still wanted to read about him.

There was nothing in the biography section, but the shop assistant took me to the poetry section and found me a copy of "Edmund Tolworth, Collected Poems and Essays 1795-1820."

Three items in hand, I went to work. In the car, I took a photo with my phone of the inside cover of Eamonn's copy of the book.

I can't say I was surprised to find that there was no sign of the man himself for the second day running. I left another voicemail, as if he wouldn't get to the other ones first, if he was even listening to them.

I returned Eamonn's copy of "The Gathering Hand" to his locker.

Clem sat with me while I put a call through to the police to report his disappearance. They took all the details and said they would investigate, asking for my number in case they needed to contact me for further information. I only told them that he hadn't turned up for work, and that I had gone over to his flat to see if he was there. I said nothing about his strange nocturnal visits to Wellowteme Crescent. Nothing of the fact that I suspected he might have been the one who tried to break into Malcolm Renfield's house. Nothing about the book, or The Tolworth Beacon. Nothing about any of it. I may live to regret it, but right then I didn't want to sound crazy.

Valerie from head office arrived at eleven with two officers from the Royalty Protection unit. Officer Tom Scanlan and Officer Richard Shearer, both looking quite sharp in their suits. Scanlan was taller with dark ginger hair, shaved almost to the scalp, Shearer was shorter with brown hair crazed with clay, both carrying themselves very much like they were from the police. Clem and I met them near the tills, offered them a paper coffee, and led them into my office to finalise the arrangements for Saturday.

Officer Scanlan sat with his chair pushed back from my desk. He was leaning forward, resting his elbows on his knees and consulting a small notebook. He had a soft Edinburgh accent, its sharper edges perhaps eroded by time spent away from that city. 'We're here to make sure everything goes smoothly on the day and to put you at ease. Everyone's coming to see the Duchess and enjoy themselves and we want to ensure that happens while keeping everyone safe. Ok?'

I nodded. Valerie said, 'Absolutely.'

'You'll start to see an increased police presence around here over the next couple of days. We'll have dogs around outside and we'll be checking bins. We'll also be checking drains and sealing them. We'll have officers here tomorrow after you close, and they'll be running a full search of the supermarket overnight. We'll need you to be around while that goes on. Notices will be going up outside to say that the car park will be cleared on Friday night to ensure we have no vehicles within five-hundred yards of the supermarket.' He looked at his colleague. 'Will you be able to have a scout round the back of the supermarket and assess what's behind it?'

Officer Shearer made some notes in his book.

Officer Scanlan continued. Once we've secured the inside of the supermarket we will have to restrict and control access until after the Duchess has departed at ten o'clock. We'll both be back on Saturday very early and you'll be able to ask us questions at any time, here is my card, just for your reassurance about anything that we're doing. So, if you have any queries or concerns you just come to me or Officer Shearer."

Officer Shearer sounded more local, more Wiltshire. He handed out his card and said. 'We'll be putting up security arches at the goods entrance for your staff at the back, so I'd recommend you advise everyone not to bring big bags into work on Saturday. We'll be doing bag searches. We'll have bag checks at the front as well for the guests arriving to come inside the supermarket. We'll also have plain clothes officers and crowd behaviour specialists outside and inside the supermarket during the event. We'll also be restricting access to the rest of the supermarket after we've completed our overnight search tomorrow and secured the space.' Consulting his notes again he said, 'We've had an instruction that there's been a change in the path that the Duchess is going to take from the entrance to where the plaque is. Is that correct?'

Valerie said, 'Yes, we've extended the guest list to include two family members of staff members and this means we've increased the length of the pathway.'

Officer Scanlan said, 'Yes no problem at all, but as it's a last-minute change we'd like to just go and have a look at where the belt-barriers will be situated. We just need to calculate that the space is sufficient to allow for the extra people. Have we been provided with an updated list of guests?'

Valerie said, 'Yes that was issued from head-office yesterday morning.'

'Great, thanks. I'll check that's been received.'

'Ok,' said Valerie, 'Shall we go around to the entrance now?'

We spent a few minutes describing the amended path route to the Royalty Protection officers, who were happy with how it was all going to be laid out.

Officer Scanlan moved the conversation on by saying. 'We need to see a couple of things if that's ok. We need to have a safe room where we can take the Duchess and other dignitaries to in the event of an emergency, and we'll need to map out the quickest path to there. Also, we'll need to define a separate exit should there be a requirement to use it, and also how we would get vehicles round to that exit if we need to.'

Steph texted as I was eating a microwave Lamb Rogan Josh for dinner, which I'd picked up from the end-of-aisle markdown shelf. It hit the spot, I think they'd changed the recipe to make it spicier and it was making me sweat in the heat. Steph's text said: *Just home from swimming. Freya's got something to tell you. Is it ok to call?*

I put my knife and fork down and tapped out a reply straight away. *Absolutely!*

Moments later the phone rang, and I answered.

Freya was giggling. 'Hi Daddy.'

'Hi my darling, how are you?' I got a sense I was on speakerphone. 'Have you got something to tell me?'

'I got Bubbles five.'

'Bubbles five! That's fantastic! What's Bubbles five darling?'

Steph said in the background, 'It's a swimming certificate.'

'A swimming certificate, that's brilliant. Well done Freya that's amazing. I'm really proud of you.'

'I'm going to be a lifeguard when I grow up.'

'Are you? Well that's a really good thing to want to be. It will be amazing if you grow up to be a special person who saves people's lives.'

'A sea lifeguard.'

'Great, and you can go to lovely beaches all around the world and make sure people are safe in the water.'

'Yeah, and if they fall out of boats I'll swim out to sea and get them.'

'But what if there are sharks?'

Then Steph obviously had the phone, taken off speaker. 'She's gone now. Still a bit young for meaningful phone conversations.'

'Yeah, wait till she's a teenager, then we won't get her off them.'

'Thanks for having her the other night.'

'No problem.'

'Everything set for Saturday?'

'Yeah. Lots to organise but we're pretty much sorted now. We met the Royalty Protection people today. Also, I was waiting for confirmation but we've had it now. I've got you and Freya onto the guest list to be inside the supermarket for the unveiling of the plaque.'

'Really? That's brilliant! Thank you for that. Freya wants to see the "Princess". It must be feeling pretty real now. With it being so imminent. Freya and I will definitely be there. Waving a Union Jack.'

'Get there early. Your names will be at the entrance.'

'Mum's planning to get down there as well.'

'I could only get two names on the list.'

'Oh, I didn't mean it like that. She'll be outside somewhere.'

I said. 'Maybe after all the fuss dies down we could take Freya for an ice-cream or something.'

She didn't answer immediately. 'Maybe. Let's see how it goes.'

◆ ◆ ◆

At eight o'clock, with two hours until the Thursday radio broadcast I sat on one of the metal folding bistro chairs on my small kitchen balcony, which overlooked a decent sized communal garden. I could smell a barbecue on the breeze. I had a glass of beer and my copy of "Edmund Tolworth, Collected Poems and Essays 1795-1820" with me.

I read some of the foreword.

Amongst those of us for whom English romantic poetry conjures images of rolling green countryside, and declarations of love at the Summer Fayre, we understand its function of the time to be an antidote to what Edmund Tolworth and his contemporaries saw to be a "dangerous world filled with both the heights and depths of opportunity and trepidation.' He was of course talking about the Industrial Revolution. Tolworth was one of the earliest advocates of Environmentalism. It was a time when hand manufacturing methods were giving way to machines. New chemicals were finding their way into factory processes. Iron was becoming a vital commodity for industry, with steam power and water power making it happen. Tolworth saw these new uses for machine tools and the mechanised factory system and despite being enthusiastic about what they had to offer, he became concerned about how it was beginning to result in, among other things, a massive wave of population expansion. Tolworth was inspired by the late eighteenth century works of Thomas Malthus and his essays on the analysis of population. And it was in the early eighteen-hundreds, when Tolworth was in his twenties, that the population of the planet hit one billion.

◆ ◆ ◆

By nine-thirty I was clear in my decision about going up to Haleswade Leap. I texted Clem. He knew about what was going on with me and Steph, so I wrote:

Need to take emergency leave tomorrow for a family matter but I'll be there in the evening before closing time. You have everything in hand but call me if you need anything.

I set up my laptop, the radio and my copy of the "The Gathering Hand" in readiness for the ten o'clock broadcast, which started to come through as soon as the clock on my phone went over from 21:59.

But at 23:22 when I'd finished I stood up from the table, stiff from sitting still for so long, and double checked I'd locked the front door. Because it said:

*OC5465DATAINTERVENTIONREQDSTOPTEMPORARYDNSRECORD
ALTERATIONOFRELAYSITESTOPSWITCHTONEWDECODEBOOKTM
INUSTWOSTOPBOOKSELECTEDUSEBOOKFOURSTOPGBDSSLFHVL
HUDSBGSDJGLBGHJVLFBHBFDHSJABHJLGFBJKAGHJFKALHHGFJK
DLAYHHDSKSDFHJKSDFHKVDSNJKASDNYFGDHCNDHFGWPRDU
NCZOWQKJK*

I switched off the lights in the flat and went to each room and closed the windows. If Eamonn was spying on me and reporting back, then that would explain why they now needed to change the decoding book. Someone knew I had a copy of "The Gathering Hand". But how did they find out? I had been so careful today.

I stood in the darkness of my bedroom, paralysed, looking down onto the night-time street. How was I being watched? Was there a recording device in my flat? A telescopic microphone pointing at me from across the street, or in the buildings at the back? Was my laptop webcam being hacked?

Shaun?

I just couldn't see it being Shaun.

Malcolm?

But he'd taken off somewhere.

If the military were involved, and given Eamonn's background I couldn't rule it out, then it wouldn't be beyond their capability to use technology to monitor my activities.

Gentlemen don't read each other's mail.

I don't know how, but somehow, they had found out about me.

FRIDAY

Anyone who lives in England knows that a week of hot weather was a rare treat, even in July. The news had been declaring it a heatwave, hotter than Spain. Pictures of white and red people crammed like sardines onto Brighton beach deckchairs. Even at seven in the morning Chalkweald was warmer than it would be mid-afternoon on most normal days. And with such a blue sky it was almost possible to convince myself I was on holiday on the continent.

I made myself a flask of coffee and threw a packet of biscuits into the car. For lunch I would probably find the nearest Hollyways to Haleswade Leap and use my staff card.

I set the Satnav, switched on the radio and drove to the garage on the way out of Chalkweald to fill up the car. Then I settled into the drive northeast. The traffic was ok on the A34 until I tried to go under the M4 motorway and then it was rush hour. So, I was slow through there. Despite the traffic the Satnav said it was still the fastest route, so I stuck with it, and after half an hour of clutch fatigue I was on my way again. Out of the window the normally green fields were starting to give way to patches of brown. Parched grass this early in summer was a rarity. On the open country road, the warm, heady breeze coming into the car, pulsing the air, was a summer sound I had real affection for.

A piece on the local radio came on about the Duchess's visit. I put the window up and turned up the volume.

...And tomorrow the Duchess will be visiting Chalkweald in Wiltshire to visit the Hollyways flagship store as part of their two-hundred-year celebrations. Now I love Hollyways. Their bakery is just terrific. Did you know that Hollyways was the first retailer to become carbon-neutral, before carbon-neutral was even a thing, and they achieved that in 1983? Now that's what I call a forward-thinking company. They have over one thousand stores around the country and a massive tree planting endeavour in areas of North Wales and the North of England as well as globally to help maintain that carbon-neutral status. We all need more of that. They were the first supermarket to put doors on their fridges. Makes a huge amount of sense. You wouldn't leave the door off your fridge at home would you, and expect to still have a small electricity bill. Hard for other supermarkets to preach about reusable plastic bags when they don't even have doors on their fridges. Anyway, good on you Hollyways. If you are planning to head down to Chalkweald to see the Duchess she's arriving at nine-thirty to meet with Dame Hollyway and store staff. But you might want to get there early. And the weather is set to be hot hot hot again so that's going to be fantastic. Onto the latest traffic news now with...

Hearing the piece about tomorrow's visit on the radio reassured me that taking the day off today, just the day before, wasn't such a reckless idea. Eamonn had been given instructions by The Tolworth Beacon directly relating to the arrangements for the visit and it was imperative that I found out why, as it could affect any part of tomorrow's festivities. I had to find out what the people behind The Tolworth Beacon were trying to orchestrate. No... *Calibrate.*

I reached Haleswade Leap National Trust car park at a quarter to eleven. I'd driven uphill about a mile from the main road through woodland to reach it. It wasn't a very big area, probably enough for twenty cars, and mostly shaded by trees. There were two cars already parked there, and one of them was Eamonn's metallic blue Peugeot. I shouldn't have been surprised to see it there, and I suppose I wasn't. But it did suddenly bring back the jarring weirdness of the situation. I parked alongside it and stopped the engine. I felt stiff from the driving, so I wasted no time in getting out into the dappled sunlight. As I was at some elevation now there was a small breeze rustling the trees and although it was still warm, it was pleasant on my face.

I poured myself a cup of coffee out of the flask and ate a shortbread biscuit. Then I picked up the Ordnance Survey map for the Haleswade Leap area. It was one of the OS Explorer Maps that said "Essential for Outdoor Activities" on the partially orange cover. Below the area information, a picture of a cyclist navigating what looked like an exposed path across the top of Haleswade Leap, a flat plain of fields and trees stretching out into the distance to his left. I flipped open the map and unfolded its concertina shape, laying it on the bonnet of my Corsa. By following from where I'd left the main road at the bottom of the hill, it didn't take long for me to locate the car park on the map.

Looking up I could see the path leading into the forested area to the northeast and I located the path on the paper, my finger traced up the path. It was a 1:25000 scale map so I was looking around eight or nine inches north of my current location for a radio mast, based on the "Three Miles North" statement on the inside cover of Eamonn's copy of "The Gathering Hand". The escarpment ran almost North-South, but not quite. I was at the south end but at the other end it widened and after a little searching I could see the radio mast symbol; a triangle with a wavy line balanced on the top. That was where I was headed. In the map there was a marked pathway starting at the car park, but it veered off and down the escarpment long before it got anywhere near the mast.

Looking further up the path I couldn't see anything looking like a radio mast from here, but mostly in the direction of Haleswade Leap which rose above me all I could see were trees. A three-mile walk would probably take a good hour. Part of me wondered as I rubbed sun cream into my face, neck and arms whether there would be any direct route to the mast at all. The map gave no indication that there was. But presumably there would be some sort of access, otherwise how would authorised people get to it, for maintenance or whatever?

I put my rucksack on my back. The path leading away from the car park was well defined and laid with sandy coloured gravel, with wooden edging. Just where it started there was a large National Trust board bearing the familiar oak leaf emblem, showing a map of the Haleswade Leap area and some of the local flora and fauna as well as a map of the walking routes that led through the area. From what I could see there was no indication that the mast was even situated on the National Trust land, as it wasn't marked on the map on the board.

The route was lined by low shrubbery and surrounded by tall trees of many varieties, mainly oaks and birch. The incline was steep at first as the path rose up towards the most elevated part of the escarpment. I stopped to take a breath a couple of times and after about ten minutes of walking the track became thinner and stonier. There were also tree roots sticking into the path. Outstretched fingers seeking to trip up anyone who wasn't paying attention.

Once the trail started to level off at the top of the escarpment I reached a gap in the trees. A wire fence lined the path to my right, overlooking the quarry to the East. The chiselled rock looked hot, devoid of shade under the high late morning sun. Although there were trucks and diggers down there, there was no activity today. No people that I could see. To my left I was greeted with the scene that the Ordnance Survey map promised. It was quite a staggering sight from up here. Miles across the flat land to the west, nothing but green fields and trees, a couple of church spires, and hardly any roads that I could see, as far as the hazy July horizon.

At this first viewpoint I stopped and took a bottle of water out of my rucksack. I had two bottles and I drank half of one now. The heat was starting to become uncomfortable and I was only wearing a t-shirt on my top half. The distant sound of motorway cars drifted across the sun-drenched fields on the warm breeze and I could hear red kites giving squeaky whistles as they twirled in the sky, riding thermals high above the escarpment.

I'd walked about a mile and the trees became denser ahead of me. There was still no sign of Eamonn or the radio mast. I pushed on, my walking shoes crunching on the dirt. I'd not come across anyone either going my way or coming the opposite way.

As I approached the dense trees towards the northern end of the escarpment I guessed I must have travelled about a mile and a half. Every now and then, when the wind changed direction, I thought I could hear a low hum. A low, electrical hum.

The sound of the hum grew a little louder as I reached the point where the pathway veered off to the left and started to descend the west side of Haleswade Leap, down towards the flattened plain beyond. I broke free of the path at this point and continued north through the shrubbery and into the woodland. I was at the highest part of the escarpment now. It had levelled off ahead of me. The shrubbery became thicker and the trees became more crowded, the thick smell of warm leaves rich in my nostrils. I walked another mile, hard-going on the uneven ground. As I did so, the hum got louder. An additional layer of sound joined the hum. A buzz.

Then I noticed it up ahead. As I made my way through the trees I saw a grey spire. A spiky, steel tower, perhaps fifty metres tall, poking above the canopy. Talismanic, talking outwards at the world through antennas mounted towards the top. At the base of the mast was a small concrete building, not much bigger than a garage. Just a box really, with a small door in the side. Between me and the door was a tall wire fence that had been strung up about twenty metres away from the mast. It appeared to surround the whole tower. A sign on the fence stated:

PRIVATE PROPERTY : KEEP OUT

Below it, a yellow and black emblem of electricity zapping a man, stating:

DANGER OF DEATH

The fence itself didn't appear to be electrified. When I reached it, I started to walk to the right along its perimeter, around the tower, crunching over dried sticks. The only other sound, apart from the buzz-hum of the mast, were crickets communicating with each other. About two-thirds of the way round the fence, I came across a hole at ground-level that had been made with wire cutters. It was big enough for a person to crawl through. I crouched down, tossed my rucksack through and made my way under the fence, taking care not to snag my t-shirt.

The breeze picked up and rustled the summer trees, peppering dappled light on the ground. I picked up my rucksack and made my way back around the wide base of the tower towards the small building. I passed a fenced-off electricity generator with another DANGER sign. The buzz-hum was pretty loud now. I made my way towards the building, over grass. I reached the wooden door, painted green. It was slightly open, so I pushed it a little. The room beyond was dark.

'Hello?' I called.

No answer. I pushed the door open fully and called again. 'Hello?'

I wasn't particularly sure about how I would explain myself if someone came out now and challenged me. Sometimes it's better not to rehearse these things but I genuinely couldn't think of a valid reason to be creeping around on this private property. Unless I made up some rubbish about owning a dog that had run off into the bushes for a crap, which seemed to work for Eamonn.

I started to move into the building, into the unlit room. I could hear an odd metallic rattling sound. My eyes began to adjust to the dark. Directly inside the door, along the wall, was a row of hooks, although no coats were hung there. At right angles to that, blocking the rest of the room was a jutting section of concrete. I navigated slowly around it. As I did so I caught sight of a leg through a wire grille. The foot was wearing a trainer, and was resting sideways on the stone floor, but the knee was elevated. The person was wearing jeans, but they weren't moving. I walked further in and despite the gloom my eyes had now adjusted, and there was enough light coming from the sunny day outside for me to see that the rest of the body belonged to Eamonn, as I had feared.

I stopped moving, because what I saw led me to believe that to take another step could kill me.

There was no doubt that Eamonn was dead. He was inside some sort of chain-link pen, with a closed cage door between us, in the nearest corner to me. He was leaning sideways into a panel of radio equipment, an old control board from a Cold War era, littered with many grey knobs, dials and needle gauges. But his lean was more of a slump, his arms dangling down, zombie-like. Because the only thing that was holding him even remotely upright was the complete mess that was his face. It took me a few seconds to comprehend exactly what I was looking at, but the side of his head was somehow fused to the radio equipment, joined to it. Skin melted onto it like wax. That appeared to be what he was hanging by. One eye had gone but the other stared vacantly at me, not seeing. Or perhaps it was seeing infinity. A metal plate was sticking out of the top of his bald head, having sliced its way out by way of what I could only imagine to be a super strong magnetic force. There were wire-cutters too, as I had guessed, no doubt pulled from his hand as he approached the equipment. They were causing the rattling sound, unsettled by the forces applied to it, balanced across an uneven surface on the control board. The magnetism must have been intensely localised, bound within the confines of the metal cage, because I couldn't feel any pull from where I stood about twelve feet away. Not from my phone or my belt or my keys.

I stepped back and back again out of the building. I tripped on the lip of the doorway and fell backwards onto my rucksack. There was nothing else in that building for me to see. I looked up at the mast. This tower. This *Beacon* had taken a life, but probably unintentionally. Why had Eamonn felt the need to come up here? I could only assume that his curiosity got the better of him. Did he even *know* who he was receiving instructions from? Did he think that by coming here he could meet the operators? His triangulation brought him here, but this was just some sort of a repeater station. The question pushed hard at me now as I'm sure it pushed hard at him, right up until the moment of his death. *Where was the broadcast really coming from?*

I got out of there. I scrambled through that hole in the fence and worked my way back around the perimeter. I wound my way through the trees, stumbling towards the relative safety of the path. All the time I could feel the transmitter behind me. Watching me. Taunting me. Telling me not to dare to come looking for answers here. There were no answers here. Go back to your ordinary life. I hiked for twenty minutes through the thick foliage and vomited in the undergrowth just shy of the path. I washed the acid from my mouth with the rest of the open water bottle and spat it across the grass. I found myself walking faster and faster to get away from that place. Soon I was running, tripping down that hill. One of the jutting tree roots got the better of me. The mast started to buzz-hum and laugh in my head as I fell forward grazing my forearm and hand as I landed. I picked myself up and pushed on.

Back at the car park I climbed into the Corsa and locked the doors. The car was hot. The seat was hot. Shimmering heat rose from the dashboard and the bonnet. I breathed hot car air, and breathed, and breathed and tried to slow my rapid heart. And the question that arose from deep within me. A question that had been there all the time but till now was suppressed by the sane mind I thought I had, was, rather than wonder *where* this broadcast was coming from, shouldn't I be wondering *when* it came from? How did the operators of this clandestine radio station know about events which had not yet happened? How could they predict events with such certainty? With the kind of predictions The Tolworth Beacon had made, the information it knew and acted upon, were these people trying to alter the course of the future. Or, more maddeningly, alter the course of the past. This transmission had been triangulated to here, a point in space, but this was not the source. Eamonn's fatal discovery here begged the question, might the source be charted to another point in time?

◆◆◆

I turned the key in the ignition, reversed out of the space and drove back down the hill to the main road. I thought about going back to the mast. But even more I thought about reporting it. Someone needed to know that Eamonn was up there. But I couldn't call the police myself, because I already had. And on what basis was I here? The reason was too complicated to explain. I could end up being a suspect. They say that murder is often committed by someone known to the victim. Someone nobody ever suspected. Well, that could be me.

What that mast did. Surely it could never be construed as murder by another human.

And what would I say at work? Would it be suspicious that I took emergency leave on the day Eamonn died? Would it even come out that he was dead? Would those responsible for the Tolworth Beacon just allow Eamonn to disappear? I'd seen enough police dramas. Without a body there was no murder, right? Either way. I knew there was a body and I knew where it was. I wasn't sure I could live with that knowledge.

I tried hard to focus on the road, but my attention kept fighting its way back to the radio mast and that horrific sight. I pulled into a layby and found myself shouting "What the fuck?!" repeatedly, banging the steering wheel in the confines of the car, tears landing on my legs.

I arrived back at Chalkweald by half past three. I had a shower at home to remove the dust that was all over me, and then I drove down to the supermarket.

◆ ◆ ◆

The queues for the tills were four or five deep at every station and the self-serve tills had a line of about fifteen. Clem was covering the area ushering people and trolleys here and there to create some space on the shop floor for those still shopping, trying to get their trolleys past. 'Lots of people are saying they want to get their shopping done today as they know it will be impossible tomorrow morning when the Duchess is here.'

They were right. With the store not opening properly until the Duchess had finished with the unveiling, people would have less time on the Saturday to get their shopping done.

Clem looked stressed, so I spent an hour with him coordinating the masses. All the time I contemplated telling him what had happened; what I had seen. But I just couldn't. I didn't know where it would lead.

Just before nine o'clock Officer Shearer arrived with a team of fifteen officers and three sniffer dogs. And after we closed they commenced their work of searching the supermarket for explosives.

I left Hollyways at nine-thirty pm. Despite my insistence, Clem offered to be on hand for the security officers first. I agreed to go back for midnight to relieve him and cover things until they'd finished. By ten o'clock I was set up next to the painting radio at home in the dining room, frosted glass of beer near at hand. God, I needed that beer. Although I knew I could pick up the broadcast via the laptop anytime, there was something primal about getting it from its source as the broadcast was happening. And besides, I wouldn't get it any sooner via the website. When the interval signal started up I was ready, and after the quaint poetry of Edmund Tolworth emanated from the small speaker, I started to write down the numbers.

By twenty past eleven I had translated the two-hundred and fifty letters to:

OC4316DETAILSOFCHALKWEALDPERPETRATORNOWAVAILABLE
BUTAREWITHHELDASITISSUSPECTEDTHATAKEYACTORMAYHAV
EACCESSTOTHESEMESSAGESSTOPOC2341ACTIVISTSHAVEINTER
VENEDINAMAZONAFFAIRITISNOWOKTODEPARTTHEAREASTOPT
EHDNCOTIGHFPSIDBCHDYSKFSHFSYHWEROQLZMZBCGFUHDGF
UEJVCSWPF

Word of a "perpetrator" was alarming. News of a key actor being in the know was even more alarming. Assuming the key actor was me, who had been tipping the Beacon operators off? If Malcolm Renfield, also known as David Wenlock, was the key actor, had Eamonn been dispatched to break into Malcolm's House across the road on Monday to find out what he knew? Did Malcolm choose to disappear? Or was he chased out? Or worse, *carried* out? Why was it whenever I had a question, the only person who could answer it would vanish?

I looked at my phone. If ever there was a time to call the police and tell them about Eamonn's body this was it.

But I couldn't. I just couldn't. If I was asked how I came to know this information I'd be stuck in an interview room for the next forty-eight hours trying to explain. And then it would be too late. I'd miss the big occasion tomorrow. I'd be interrogated to reveal my sources. If it came to light that I didn't report finding Eamonn earlier today, at the time when I found him, not eight hours later, my problems would be compounded further. It was like our car crash in Tilmere Woods. Like Freya. There comes a point when it's just too late to come clean. But I didn't like how it made me feel, to withhold all of this. It made me feel sick. And still I kept seeing the image of Eamonn's one eye staring into some distant abyss.

I would keep a close eye on things tomorrow. Also, there would be a whole team of plain-clothes officers and I was sure there would be plenty of uniformed police there too. I couldn't tip them off to a perpetrator. They'd want to know everything.

Hopefully I could rely on them tomorrow. It was their job to make sure things went smoothly, no matter what The Tolworth Beacon had in store.

Exhausted, but still more than a little wary about the subject of the broadcast, I shut all the windows and curtains in the flat, leaving only one window open on the latch in the bedroom to let in whatever cool air the night decided to push at it. I sat at the dining table with my laptop. I opened my Web browser and navigated to TOLWORTH-RELAY.NET but all I was getting was a PAGE NOT FOUND error. I WhatsApp'd Shaun, and he replied almost immediately saying his page had been having problems all day. Something about DNS records not refreshing and that he was trying to get it restored. If only I had copied down the numbers earlier in the week from his website, then I could have done the decoding offline. I knew there was little point in revisiting the first set of numbers that I'd taken down on the sticky notes and transferred to my phone on Tuesday night, as Freya had interrupted me, and I ended up missing what might have amounted to a third of the total message.

There was nothing more to do. So, I drove back down to Hollyways to relieve Clem.

When I arrived at the supermarket at midnight I would have been forgiven for thinking it was still open, such was the level of activity. I met Clem at the entrance for a handover. Two sniffer dogs were traversing the aisles accompanied by officers and I saw a third dog emerge from the door to the offices. Officers were looking through clothes racks, behind books, moving milk around in the fridges. All sorts of checks were being carried out by the search team.

'They're being unbelievably thorough. If there's an IED in here, they'll find it.'

'IED?'

Clem gave a smug smile. 'Yeah a bomb. An Improvised Explosive Device.'

I clapped my hand on his upper arm. 'Ha, get you with the lingo! Two hours in here and you're ready to join the police force.'

'I think you're in for at least another two hours. After that they're going to secure the building and station guards around the place. You'll be good to go and get some kip after that.'

'Well, you do that now please, and come back down here at about six if you can.'

'Sure thing.'

I was about to say something about Haleswade Leap, but instead just said. 'Thank you so much for today Clem. I really appreciate all you've done to support me this week.'

'No problem Chris. We'll be able to get a proper night's sleep after tomorrow.'

'Yes,' I said, nodding, 'In a way I'm looking forward to it all being over and done with.'

After Clem left I headed round to the staff room to get a paper coffee. The fluorescents were slightly dimmer in here, which provided some relief for my eyes at this late hour.

Officer Shearer was in there drinking a cup of his own. 'Hi. Have you taken over from Clem?'

'Clem looked tired. You guys must be like tireless robots.' I walked over to the coffee machine.

'I've got a couple of questions if that's ok?'

I pressed the button for a Cappuccino. 'Absolutely, ask away.'

'We'll need to station one of our officers at your CCTV screen tomorrow throughout the event.'

'Ok that's no problem, we have it on a computer system which you can access from either Clem's desk or mine. You may as well use mine.'

Officer Shearer nodded. 'Ok, fantastic. I'll introduce you to the officer we'll be stationing there, he's on the supermarket floor at the moment. Now, understandably you have a number of items in the supermarket which could be used in a dangerous manner. You have glassware, cutlery, lighter fluid, plus any number of things that could be used as projectiles. And while all the guests have been vetted, we have to be prepared for any eventuality.'

An image formed in my head of someone lobbing potatoes at the Duchess from the vegetable aisle. I tried very hard not to smile in front of Officer Shearer. But he was right. A supermarket had all manner of things that could be used dangerously. And until a situation like this, I hadn't really given that a moment's thought.

'So, once we've completed the search tonight and put the place into lockdown, we'll have officers on sentry duty throughout the rest of the night and into the morning. But when the guests arrive tomorrow we'll have some officers restricting access to the aisles. In other words, we don't want anyone venturing deeper into the shop and potentially getting access to things.'

'Ok,' I said. 'Where will the restricted area start?'

'Everyone will be around the belt-barriers where the fruit will be so beyond that we'll have officers stopping people going elsewhere in the supermarket. There's also going to be two media pens. One outside but a smaller one inside for the local press as they're pushy, they'll all want to get pictures of the Duchess unveiling the plaque.'

The search was complete at two o'clock. We closed up the supermarket and officers took up sentry duty. It was still a warm evening but just a tiny bit fresher than usual. I took a full deep breath. It was a pleasant feeling to inhale the night air so completely.

I was tired now. I made my way over to my Corsa and paused by the door before I got in. The town of Chalkweald was practically silent. All I could hear were the distant cars on the bypass, and a low conversation between two officers by the entrance to the supermarket.

Looking up at the sky, a beautiful band of stars scarred the night. I was gazing towards the centre of the Milky Way from the humble car park of Hollyways supermarket.

What broadcasts were travelling over my head right now? What message were the operators of The Tolworth Beacon preparing for their next broadcast? And what book would be required to decrypt it?

And Eamonn. What to make of Eamonn, whose final resting place was the top of a wooded escarpment seventy-five miles from here? I could only hope that one day I would understand fully his role in all of this.

I got in the car and drove home to get what little sleep I could.

At two-twenty I was lying in bed. It was going to be quite a day, so I switched off the light and tried to get to sleep. I flipped over a hundred times. I couldn't settle. Not with all these thoughts.

Even as I lay there staring at the ceiling I wondered what I would do if I got up, parted the curtains and saw Eamonn standing down there on Wellowteme Crescent, like he had on Tuesday night. Watching the house. Like some automaton doing The Tolworth Beacon's bidding.

That nightmarish image stayed with me, and it was three o'clock before I eventually fell asleep.

SATURDAY

I didn't sleep long, barely an hour. It may have been a warm night but that wasn't the reason. It was nerves. At four o'clock I got up and walked around the flat. I got myself a glass of water, drank it down in one, then opened the curtains in my room.

Eamonn wasn't standing across the road.

I got back into bed and lay there, staring out of the window as the earliest tinge of dawn crept into the sky and the planets rotation continued to bring the sun around to our side.

When the last of the stars disappeared, I got out of bed again and went to get a shower. Clean, I felt less tired, but there was still anxiety, still this deep feeling in my core that this day was going to be even bigger than I was already anticipating. Not only was it huge for my career, to be the General Manager of the flagship Hollyways supermarket when the company was celebrating its two-hundredth anniversary. To get an opportunity to meet royalty. That was big. But all this "Perpetrator" business... this *Eamonn* business?

When I got out of the shower I saw my phone had a notification. It was Shaun telling me his website was back up and he'd uploaded the section of the radio broadcast that had been missed while the site was down. Well, I didn't need that section of the broadcast. I needed the broadcasts that came earlier in the week, and now that they were accessible I didn't have the time to sit down and decode them because I had to get back to the supermarket.

I put on my best navy suit, a light blue shirt brand new out of a packet and hastily ironed, and a dark blue tie. I ate breakfast at just after four-thirty.

By five o'clock I was parked up again at the supermarket, as though I had never left. It occurred to me to delete the journey to Haleswade from my Satnav history. So, I did that before I got out of the car. At the goods entrance there was a police team putting together a Security arch and bag-checking table. An officer came over to check my car over.

I met Clem and Max by the goods entrance and Clem handed me a paper coffee. 'Saw you pull up.'

'Thanks,' I said. 'Are we nervous?'

Max nodded and sipped his coffee. Clem said, 'Actually yes I am. Big day.'

My phone pinged. It was a Facebook Direct Message from Mike the Vault. *Good luck today. Hope to see you on the news!*

Good luck indeed. If only he knew how much I really would need it. I replied with a simple: *Thanks Mike!*

'It's going to be quite something,' I said to the guys. 'Come on, shall we go in?'

Clem and Max followed me through the goods entrance and we walked together to the front of the supermarket. We met Officer Tom Scanlan there. He was starting to put out the belt-barriers in the updated configuration, the one that meandered more, nearer to the first island of fruit, on its way from the entrance to the plaque unveiling area, so as to allow the additional guests to fit inside. This was the configuration that The Tolworth Beacon instructions appeared to be trying to engineer, or *Calibrate*? At least that was how it seemed from what I had been able to ascertain. I contemplated asking for it to be changed back to the straighter path, to eliminate whatever it was these mysterious instructions were supposed to achieve, but given the chain of command and approval that had been needed for even the slightest detail over the last few weeks I knew that we were not going to be changing anything on the actual morning of the visit.

And besides, as the idea had been conveyed to upper management by me, I was going to look daft asking to renege on it.

Clem and I helped with the belt-barriers to construct the path and the media pen, and at a quarter to seven Valerie appeared. Normally quite collected, her eyes seemed to be scanning everywhere and everything quickly in a way that seemed to betray her escalating nerves. She had her rucksack with her and she kept unnecessarily adjusting the strap's position on her shoulder.

At seven o'clock I stepped outside the front and took in a deep breath of warm summer air. I told myself I didn't need it, but my nerves were starting to quicken my heart rate, and having an opportunity to pace outside was a good way to pass the time, and give an outlet for pent-up energy. After all the preparations over the last few days, weeks and months, everything was in place, and there was nothing else to be done except pace about. The sun was getting high now and really beginning to deepen the warmth of the day, by reheating the stone, metal and concrete here that had not had a chance to fully cool down overnight. Above the entrance to the supermarket the massive Hollyways logo presided, resplendent in purple, with the familiar leafy tree sticking out the top of the capital H, its metal trim glinting in the rising sunlight.

I texted Steph. *Hi, you might want to think about getting down here, it's getting busy.*

I looked round at the two cleaners, Cerys was giving the entrance hall a sweep. The other cleaner was spraying and wiping the glass windows and doors around the entrance hall.

My phone pinged. Steph replied. *Ok thanx for the heads-up. We're on our way.*

I saw Officer Shearer directing two reporters from the Chalkweald Echo over to the specially designated media pen just near the main entrance. He was also talking on his mobile phone.

Clem came out and brought me a paper coffee. 'Still nothing from Eamonn?'

I shook my head. 'I've reported it.'

'Really strange that. Not like him at all to just do a disappearing act.'

I looked at Clem. 'Did he ever talk about anyone? Mates, girlfriend, family?'

Clem took a sip of coffee. 'Come to think of it, not that I can ever recall.'

'Me neither. Never seemed all that odd, till now.'

We stood together and watched the activity. The car park was not open for public vehicles, and two officers in yellow hi-vis jackets were standing at the car park entrance directing traffic accordingly. In one corner of the car park were two police vans and an ambulance. I could see paramedics and officers grouped together beside them, chatting. I could see other police officers near the entrance to Hollyways, near the media pen. One of them was the tall, thin officer from the suspected burglary on Wellowteme Crescent in the early hours of Monday.

A BBC Outside Broadcast lorry arrived, satellite dishes on its roof pointing all the way to the blue sky. Two other men in hi-vis jackets, car park attendants operating inside the car park, drafted in by Hollyways head office, directed the van towards the opposite corner from where the police vans and the ambulance were parked, but nearer to the supermarket.

Lots of people were gathering near the barriers at the entrance to the supermarket, but I still hadn't seen Steph, her Mum Katrina or Freya.

Clem said, 'All these people, and none of them are actually going to be leaving with any shopping.'

'Just think of the publicity. That's all we need to worry about today.'

At eight forty-five staff from the store were handing out the Anniversary Celebration Vouchers and Leaflets to members of the public around the entrance. I went back inside, through the security arch and past the lady from the Royal Media Team who was checking off the names on the guest list as people arrived. I saw that Steph and Freya had already pitched up. They were in a spot just inside the entrance of the supermarket. It occurred to me again that had it not been for the barrier reconfiguration and extra guests that Eamonn had suggested, then they wouldn't have been able to get inside. So I was pleased about that. I went to see them from my privileged position inside the barriers. Steph had had a load of her dark red hair chopped off. She was wearing it in a bob. Funny, I'd always asked her to wear it like that, but she never did. She wore a flowing blue maxi-dress and a chunky necklace of large teal beads. Freya looked like she'd fallen out of a Boden catalogue, in a yellow floral summer dress, hair tied back with a clip with a big daisy on it. I picked her up and kissed her temple. She let me hold her for about ten seconds then wriggled to be put down.

'Nervous?' said Steph.

'My mouth is dry.'

She picked up her handbag from the floor. 'Want some water?'

I shook my head. 'I'll get some in a minute.'

'Mum's outside with some friends.'

Clem called my name. He was over by the plaque. I said goodbye to Steph and Freya and went over to where he was.

He was with Officer Shearer. The Officer said, 'Do we have anyone who can move these back a bit?' He was referring to the charity token boxes, the ones where people vote for which local cause Hollyways should donate to. Looking at the big Perspex box, it did look like it might get in the way once a crowd was here around the plaque.

'I'll get a couple of lads from Deliveries to shift it,' said Clem, and he disappeared down the cosmetics aisle.

At nine o'clock the top brass arrived through the front entrance. Our CEO (the youngest ever) Phil Weare and his wife. The Deputy Chairman Gregory Lane and *his* wife. Then there was Rose Fisher, the Head of Finance and her husband. These six would be lined up near the plaque. I would be there too with Clem, and two members of staff, Ann Buckland from the tills and Mark Penn from Deliveries, both of whom had won a prize draw three months earlier to be present in the welcome line to meet the Duchess.

I scanned the people lined up by the barriers, not only to see if I could spot this perpetrator that the Tolworth Beacon referred to, but to try to detect who in the crowd were plain-clothes officers. I have to say, all were chameleonic.

At ten past nine I saw Valerie wheeling Marianne Evans out to the front of the store. Marianne was ninety-six and was the oldest living employee of Hollyways, she retired thirty years ago. Thin and frail with the whitest curly hair, and confined to a wheelchair, tartan blanket across her legs, she always wore a smile. She was positioned just near where the cars would stop and would be among the first to meet the Duchess when she arrived.

I popped over, shook her hand and said, 'Mrs Evans I'm glad you're here, one of the checkout staff has called in sick.'

This prompted a laugh. 'Good heavens Mr Powell, you'll not get me back on those tills.'

She hadn't actually worked at this branch, she'd been a till lady at the one in Shrewsbury for forty-eight years, and was quite the celebrity, and was often utilised by the supermarket on promotional material when the company wanted to market to the older, traditional customer demographic. The grey pound. If I turned out to be as alert as her when I hit ninety-six I'd be pretty happy.

I caught a glimpse out through the main entrance at the staggering number of people outside, and a bunch of photographers and camera operators in the media pen. There were also a couple of cameramen free of the pen, presumably preparing to film the Duchess and her cohorts getting out of the car when they arrived.

At nine twenty there was still no sign of a perpetrator. Officer Scanlan ushered us over to the area by the plaque and we all lined up like school kids. 'The Duchess is ten minutes away.'

In the line-up I was first, followed by Clem, then the two prize-draw winners, both wearing those on-brand purple "Hollyways two-hundred" sash things we got, then Valerie, then four of the six in the top brass crowd who had arrived together, the only two who weren't lined up with us were Phil Weare, the CEO, and his wife. Officer Scanlan had taken them outside to greet the Duchess and Dame Hollyway as they got out of their cars, Dame Hollyway in the first car and the Duchess in the second. We were lined up with our backs to the indoor guests, facing the wall where the curtain covered plaque hung. Behind us, behind the barriers were the one-hundred guests who were all here to see the Duchess, catch her eye, point their mobile phone cameras at her, and fawn over what fashion choices she had made, and how she had done her hair.

Clem nudged me and said. 'It just occurred to me. I never moved those fruit shelves the other day. After the CCTV of that guy dropping his items on the floor.'

I looked at him. 'Didn't you?'

'I never checked we'd picked everything up from underneath. Slipped my mind with all the stuff about Eamonn going missing.'

A strange hush started to fall over the assembled guests, as though by telepathy they had found out that the Duchess's car had arrived. Perhaps friends were texting from outside. I looked over at where Steph and Freya were, and their heads were pointing the other way, towards the entrance, waiting for that first glimpse. I could hear cheering outside.

And now I was crapping myself.

The cheering carried on for a couple of minutes without much else happening. There was no sign of anyone, and pretty much all of us inside the supermarket were watching the entrance, waiting for the Duchess and Dame Hollyway to appear, but presumably they were talking to Marianne Evans and members of the public.

I was about to lean over and say something more to Clem

about the fruit shelving, but the clapping and cheering started up inside the entrance and I didn't get the chance. Officers Scanlan and Shearer came in first, radios clipped to their hips, followed by Dame Hollyway and the Duchess, the Mayor and the council leader, and then Phil Weare and his wife. Flags started waving and more cheering rose amongst the rest of the congregated guests inside.

The Duchess was wearing a stylish white flowing full-length dress that was off the shoulders, with what looked like thin grey pinstripes on it. She wore sparkling heels that probably came from somewhere like Jimmy Choos and she was carrying a small grey clutch bag. I'm sure all these things would be imitated and sold on the High Street within the week. And it was inciting gushes of "Isn't she beautiful" from the ladies that were stood near me. And she was. Behind her, near the door, a man with a TV camera resting on his shoulder pointed his lens our way.

I caught sight of some litter on the floor. It looked like packaging and, absurdly, as I was less than five seconds away from meeting the Duchess, I thought, I hope they paid for that before they opened it.

But the tills were closed.

Then she was standing in front of me, looking at me with a huge disarming smile. Dame Hollyway said, 'This is Chris Powell our General Manager.' I bowed slightly and shook the Duchess's hand.

'Congratulations to you,' she said. 'What a time to be working with such a progressive company.'

I smiled through the nerves, and nodded, 'Thank you. It's an honour to be here and to meet you. This is my deputy Clem Chambers.'

She shook Clem's hand next to me and as they started to talk a rising fizzing crackling sound came from outside the entrance to the supermarket. It was so loud that everyone turned, including the Duchess, to see what the commotion was. It sounded like fireworks. Definitely fireworks, going off somewhere outside. Cracking and whistling and causing gasps from the crowd beyond the doors. A couple of plain clothes officers emerged from the throng inside the supermarket (*now* I could see them!) and ducked under the belt-barriers before heading off towards the entrance.

I caught sight of that litter on the floor again, and in that moment, I realised that it was the torn open packaging of one of Hollyways finest "Sharp Forever" kitchen knives. I looked up from it and realised that while everyone was staring in the direction of the entrance, wondering what the fireworks were all about, I was staring right into the face of a thin man, blonde-haired with sunken cheeks. He was using the knife to cut the belt-barrier. The knife he had just unwrapped from its packaging. With the aisles on lockdown and no one being allowed deeper into the shop due to the police presence restricting access behind the crowd I could only surmise that it had been smuggled in.

Impossible. There's a security arch.

But then I realised that I had seen the man before. The blonde hair and thin face. I recognised him from the CCTV footage that Clem and I had been watching earlier in the week. We'd just been talking about him. He was the man who had accidentally dropped his shopping in the fruit aisle. Cerys, the cleaner, hadn't picked it all up, had she? And Clem hadn't moved the shelves to check.

He was through the barrier in seconds. He stepped forward towards the Duchess, trying to come around me. I didn’t really know how to react to this and I wasn’t even thinking but I leaned towards him, blocking his approach, accidentally but perhaps not accidentally shoving the Duchess aside in the process. And still most people’s attention seemed to be on the firework commotion at the entrance. The Duchess made a strange gasp, expressing complete surprise. But I wasn’t facing her. I reflexively did a weird upwards arm movement that knocked the knife in the man’s hand, causing him to almost drop it but not quite. At the very least he had to change his grip on it, resulting in him grasping it pathetically at the end of the handle between his thumb and index finger in a way that wouldn’t be very effective if he were to try to use it. He was wearing chinos and a plain blue shirt, the fabric of which was thin enough for me to see the tattooed outline of a swastika on his upper arm. He smelled of musty, days-old aftershave. I made a *hmph!* noise as I tried to shove him, but he was already dodging away. Then Officer Scanlan was there, trying to grab him by the arm, but instead catching only the body of his shirt. The man launched himself off me, pushing into my chest hard with his free hand. He started to run away along the route towards the entrance, yelling at the top of his voice.

'Climate change is a LIE!' he shouted into the crowd, but I don't think anyone heard him over the sound of the fireworks.

I watched him darting towards the doors, only just about managing to stay on his feet. I caught sight of Freya, having seen the danger I had been in, breaking free of Steph without her noticing. I had no idea what our girl was thinking. She started running towards me. The blonde-haired man had taken a slightly arced trajectory along the route towards the entrance.

'*This place profits because you stupid people believe it!*' he yelled, still brandishing the knife.

Someone screamed. More people were turning their heads towards this new development. Freya was still running and her direct line to me intersected the blonde-haired man's curving path to the doors. He had gone into a full charge, a guttural roar spewing from him. Spittle and rage. Then everyone was looking. Scanlan was in pursuit, using his radio to request assistance. The man collided with Freya. Being so much lighter than him, her forward movement quickly turned into a sideways fall as his greater momentum knocked her off course. She almost seemed to crumple. It was like watching a teddy bear getting caught under the wheels of a car. He barrelled over her, his feet missing her I think, but still going forward. The collision had knocked him off balance. He stumbled and lost his footing, threw his arms out, still holding the knife, but holding it properly now. It had blood on it.

Steph was trying to push forward. I could see her beyond this mess trying to get under the belt-barrier, not managing very well. There was shouting and people surging forward elsewhere, and others retreating. Those coming forward pushed the barriers over and rushed towards the man as he fell to the ground, and the plain-clothes officers were there. On him. Freeing the knife. Subduing him. Rolling him onto his front. Arm up his back. And all the time he was shouting *'The truth will come out. Don't let them blind you with lies...!'*

'Stop resisting!' the officer yelled. 'Stop....RESISTING!"

His knee was on the blonde-man's back and that winded him sufficiently that he stopped shouting.

Officer Shearer was leading the Duchess and the Mayor towards the alternative exit. I watched them for a moment until I heard a woman yell. 'She's bleeding!'

Then I heard Steph scream 'NO!' so loudly that it seemed to bounce and echo off the walls despite the commotion. She skidded onto her knees beside Freya. Beside our girl. I was there a second later and Officer Scanlan was with us. He was already on his radio calling for medical assistance. Freya was crying and there was blood. A lot of it. The knife had caught her upper left arm and scored a few inches down it. There was a pool on the floor, reflecting the fluorescent lights on the ceiling.

Officer Scanlan was kneeling next to Freya and his hands were on the wound. He was closing it up. A pile of grey t-shirts with the tags on landed next to him. He took one and bound it round her arm, 'Thanks.' Then two paramedics were parting the crowd, arriving with bags. I saw them move Valerie and Phil Weare to one side. They were kneeling, taking over, getting to work. Steph and I, and Officer Scanlan were being moved aside by I don't know who to let the pros do what they do best. I lost sight of Freya then because they'd closed around her as she lay crying on the floor. She was the epicentre of a small crowd of kneeling paramedics and police officers. She was the epicentre, and this was seismic. An earthquake to rupture our foundations. I say ours, because my hand was being clawed at, squeezed and kneaded. It was Steph's hand and I threw my arms around her. I clawed her in return. Because the two of us were falling down a fissure in the world, and clawing our way out together was the only way through this unfolding madness.

There were people everywhere and I noticed sirens now.

A team of officers were blocking the entrance while a small cordon was being placed around the spent fireworks. They were not allowing people out through the main entrance to the supermarket. Guests were being directed like traffic towards the alternative exit. The barriers were being dismantled by police officers. Clem was standing nearby, he seemed immobilised. Over Steph's shoulder he and I looked at each other in disbelief. I had no idea at that moment if he had recognised the blonde-haired man. I released Steph and looked around, but I couldn't see the perpetrator and I'm glad I didn't because all I wanted to do was let my hot hot blood power me over to where he was and kick the living shit out of him. But he was bound to be in the back of a wagon by now.

'Chris, they're asking for her blood type?' It was Officer Scanlan. He was starting to move towards the doors. It had only been a few seconds, but Freya had been transferred onto a stretcher and was already heading towards the alternative exit. Steph and I hurried behind, out of Hollyways into the open, where a path was being cleared ahead of the stretcher by police and helpers. People being held back under the hot, bright, uncomfortable sun.

Siren sounds overlapped.

The ambulance had been driven to the alternative exit and Officer Scanlan saw us quickly into the back of it with the stretcher. We were told to sit on a bench on the right-hand side while the paramedics continued to work on Freya on the left side of the vehicle. Steph held her hand and was repeating 'We're with you. Mummy and Daddy are here. You're going to be fine.'

There was a mask over Freya's face. One young female paramedic told us that they were giving her something to calm her as she had been fighting them.

'We're getting her to hospital,' Steph said quietly. 'We're getting her to hospital. Aren't we?'

'This time we really are,' I heard myself whisper.

At Chalkweald Hospital they rolled her straight into theatre. Steph and I weren't allowed to follow but a female doctor approached us wearing green hospital uniform. She was short, tanned, with warm eyes and long sandy hair in a ponytail. She was carrying a clipboard and she said. 'My name is Sophie Dent. I'm the lead paediatric surgeon here. I'm going to examine and operate on your daughter.' Looking at Steph she said. 'She's getting prepped for surgery now. I need to ask you to sign this consent form.'

Steph nodded 'Yes of course.' She took the clipboard. Her hand was shaking. She tried to unclip the pen from the bulldog clip at the top and fumbled it, dropping it to the floor.

I picked it up and gave it to her.

Sophie put her hand on Steph's forearm. 'She's in very safe hands. We're going to look after her.'

'Take a breath,' I said, putting my arm around her.

Steph breathed out, and then in. Sophie indicated where on the page to put the pen and Steph scribbled her signature.

Taking the clipboard, Sophie said, 'I'll come and speak to you soon.'

While we were waiting in the busy corridor a young man in a white shirt and black waistcoat bounded up to us, holding his mobile phone up.

'I'm from the Chalkweald Post. Have you got a moment to talk about your daughter? They're saying she's a hero.'

Steph was fighting tears, so I started to speak, but almost immediately a police officer grabbed the man by the upper arm and wheeled him away. 'Not a good time mate. Not a good time at all.'

Another officer said, 'Can you both come with me?'

Steph's phone pinged. I don't think she heard it. We followed the officer back down the corridor into a private room. It looked like it might be a room used for delivering bad news. It had two functional blue sofas, a small table with fake lillies in a jar, and a window looking out onto a small courtyard garden. 'Just wanted to get you some privacy,' he said.

'Will the doctors know we're here?' said Steph.

'I'll make sure they know.' He stepped out of the room and closed the door.

'*Chris!*' Steph's eyes were slits as though closing them was going to stop the flow of helpless tears. And I couldn't manage to be strong either because our Freya was so vulnerable and so fragile and if that was it... if that was it... If we'd had all we were going to have of her and after that it would just be photos and videos and fading memories and a bedroom we'd freeze in time, then where did that leave us? Where do you go from that?

We waited. It was an eternal wait. We stood, we paced. Steph texted her Mum. We sat. Steph continued to knead my hand with a strength that I thought would break it, but I let her because I didn't care if she broke it. Anything to allow her to get through this moment.

Her phone pinged again. She ignored it.

We'd been in there an hour. When the door opened, Steph and I stood up. Sophie Dent walked in. Officer Scanlan followed carrying two cups of what was probably tea, which he put down on the table. I held my breath.

'I've just finished operating on Freya. Your daughter is fine. The injury she sustained was a long cut, but it wasn't deep. We've done an x-ray and it didn't go near the humerus and there's no nerve damage that we can see. We've stitched her up and as it was a clean cut I'm confident it will heal with minimal scarring. As you know she was given blood on the way here.'

It was a blur to me. I hadn't noticed them do that.

Steph exhaled, I pulled her close to me. She shuddered. I rubbed her bare arms. Sophie Dent continued. 'Officer Scanlan had expressed some concern over the radio that she may have been stepped on. On review of the x-ray and a thorough examination I'm pleased to say there is no evidence of that happening.'

'Can we see her?' Steph said.

Sophie nodded. 'We've got her in a room but she's asleep. We put her under. It'll be a couple of hours before she wakes up. But yes, you can see her.'

◆ ◆ ◆

We were led deeper into the hospital to a private room where our pale daughter lay sleeping. She was hooked up to a pulse monitor and was receiving fluids through an IV line into her uninjured right arm. Her arms lay on top of the lime green bed clothes.

Sophie Dent and Officer Scanlan left us alone with Freya. We both took chairs next to the bed, Steph nearer to Freya than me. She stroked Freya's cheek.

'You think you have one job,' Steph whispered. 'To get them as far as adulthood without getting them killed.'

I finished what she was thinking, 'You just have to hope that you win more battles than the universe does.'

She nodded.

I continued. 'It may not look like it now, but we won this one too.'

◆ ◆ ◆

Freya woke at six o'clock. Groggy, contemplating whether to look at the world. Her eyes seemed to spend a minute adjusting. She was trying to understand why she couldn't rationalise where she was when she was put out, with where she was now. She was about to cry, but she eventually saw us in the room and managed to fight it back. Nurses were there. But they didn't appear to need to check anything specific about Freya.

Steph squeezed her daughter's good right hand and leaned over to kiss her cheek.

'Hello you.'

'How are you feeling?' I said.

Through cracked lips she said, 'I didn't like that man.'

The nurse held a cup of water to her mouth and she sipped.

'None of us did. He was a bad man,' I said.

'He didn't hurt the Princess, did he?'

'The Princess is fine.'

Sophie opened the door. 'Someone told me there was a brave girl in here. Has anyone seen a brave girl? Have I come to the right place?'

Freya started giggling. 'Me!'

'Well, everyone wants to know who you are. And I do mean everyone!'

Steph's phone pinged again. She looked at it. 'It's Mum. She's out front.'

While Sophie attended to Freya, I left Steph with her and went out to fetch Katrina. Katrina with her jet-black hair which she wore spiky and up like Liza Minelli, and orange leathery skin that had been too many times in a tanning salon as well as the real sun. I bent down to her and she hugged me tight, a wide hooped earring batting the side of my face. A very sweet perfume hit my nostrils.

'It was quite a cut Katrina, but the paediatric surgeon says there's no lasting harm. It didn't go to a bone, and they think it will heal well. She's awake now.'

Katrina let out a huge sigh, a sigh that clearly exiled several hours of the tension of not knowing.

'I was outside near where the fireworks went off. People were saying that there was a knife man in there running rampant threatening people.'

'It wasn't quite like that.'

'I had no idea that you'd been involved, and Freya, until one of your colleagues came out. Clem. I saw him and approached him. He looked shell-shocked. I'd spoken to him many times before in the shop, so he knew you were my son in law. It made the one o'clock news. They're calling you a hero. And because they know she's your daughter…'

We walked back through to Freya's room, and grandmother and mother held each other hard for a good while.

'I wish Dad was here too,' said Steph. But he wasn't, and he hadn't been for eleven years. Although I'd never met him, when I thought of her Dad and why he wasn't there it made me think of that seat belt he forgot to put on. And when I thought of that, of seat belts not worn, I came right back round to Freya.

Katrina waved for me to leave the room with her. 'I just need to borrow Chris,' she said to her daughter.

We left Steph with Freya and stood in the corridor just outside. Katrina put a hand on my upper arm and spoke quietly. 'You look exhausted. I'm sure you've had a hell of a week, not to mention today. Why don't you go and get some sleep? Freya's obviously ok. I'll stay with Steph for now. One of us will call you if anything changes.'

'Maybe just for a few hours. Then I can come back down.'

'I don't know what happened between you two. I don't know what caused her to come and live with me these last three weeks. I don't *want* to know. But whatever it is I hope it's temporary, for your daughter's sake.'

◆ ◆ ◆

Steph was going to stay in the hospital overnight. They got her a camp bed to put next to Freya's.

She promised to call me if the situation changed.

Tom Scanlan met me in the corridor and said, 'I'll drive you back to the supermarket to get your car. Or would you rather go straight home?'

'No, I'll pick up my car, that's fine.'

'Will you be ok to drive?'

'I'm only a few minutes away. I'm tired but I'll be ok.'

'There's press out the front. The police commissioner has given them a statement. You are likely to encounter the media now. For now, don't say anything to them.'

'Understood.'

'We need to go out through a back entrance. My car is waiting there.'

◆ ◆ ◆

As I pulled into Wellowteme Crescent it was beginning to get dark and it was still very warm. My driver's side window was down, and I could smell barbeques in the evening air again. About two hundred yards from my building I was flagged down by a police officer who stepped partially into the road. I stopped next to him and lowered the passenger side window.

'Good evening Mr Powell. Sorry to bother you. Officer Scanlan texted ahead to let me know you were on your way. I just wanted to let you know that there are some journalists and photographers standing outside your home. I can't stop them from being there, but I can assist you with getting access to your front door. I have a couple of other officers with me who will be intervening if anyone gets in your way.'

'Thank you, officer. What should I say to them?'

Looking ahead up the road he said, 'Don't say anything.'

I drove on and as I pulled up outside my building, I saw the small crowd of about ten people next to the path beside my building. Standing slightly away from them, leaning against the building with his arms folded, was another man, clearly not wishing to be a part of the main group. When my headlights lit him up I realised it was Malcolm Renfield.

I parked alongside him and got out. 'Do I call you Malcolm, or David?'

He seemed genuinely surprised. 'I assumed you might have some questions. But it sounds like you know more than I thought.'

And then the rest of the crowd realised it was me and started to make their approach.

'I'm exhausted,' I said. 'But I know I won't sleep. You'd better come inside.'

As we headed towards my building we said nothing to the reporters but of course we couldn't stop the photographers taking pictures.

'Mr Powell are you aware that the nation is calling you and

your daughter heroes?'

'Has the Duchess contacted you?'

'How is your daughter?'

'Did the attacker say anything to you?'

The two police officers stepped forward. One said, 'Come on let the man get to his home.'

I offered Malcolm a beer. He accepted, and we sat on my small balcony off the kitchen, which faced the communal garden at the back of the building. We caught the last of the evening's warmth. The smell of freshly cut lawn was carried on the breeze. An intoxicating summer smell. Somewhere, through a distant open window, I could hear the laughter and clapping of a Saturday night gameshow.

Malcolm was wearing a red and blue plaid shirt and jeans. His attire and his white hair gave him the look of a Country and Western singer. But the thing that betrayed that image was his hard, East London accent.

'Mind if I smoke?'

'Not at all.'

'This'll be on the front pages tomorrow.'

'I have a lot to ask you.'

'Maybe I can help you with some of the answers. But I have a couple of questions myself.'

'I'll help you where I can. But Malcolm, where do you fit into all this?'

He took a cigarette packet out of the breast pocket of his shirt, pulled a cigarette and a lighter out from inside the pack and lit one. Savouring the smoke, then exhaling, he seemed to be looking for a place to begin.

Momentarily contemplating his rather smart looking brown boots, he eventually said. 'I've been listening to Numbers Stations for twenty years. I've been fascinated by these... these one-way conversations traversing the globe, over all our heads, providing information and instructions to people in hiding. The sound of them. Numbers through the static. Sends shivers it does. I used to live in London, and I spent a lot of time as a kid listening into police band chatter on the AM dial, and people's cordless phone conversations if they were within two hundred metres. And in the city, that's a lot of people. I was lucky enough to come into a substantial sum of money when I was in my early twenties. My parents died abroad. They were oil workers in Nigeria and were caught up in a tribal shooting incident in Port Harcourt. In the seventies.'

'I'm sorry.'

Malcolm uttered a small laugh. 'We didn't get on. But I had no brothers or sisters and they owned three houses, two in London. So, I inherited. When money stopped being an object I decided to pursue my ever-growing fascination with Numbers Stations and radio cryptography, and power of sound in spy craft. I was fascinated by something I heard somewhere when I was quite young. Someone told me that during World War Two, the chimes of Big Ben on the radio were not broadcast live but were a recording. Sonic interpretation was so sophisticated that the Germans could tell, from the live sound of Big Ben on the radio, what the weather was like in London, which told them whether the conditions were suitable for a bombing run. This little fact blew my mind when I was a twelve-year-old child learning about the darker side of humanity, and the tactics of conflict. Once I heard that fact, I was hooked. Later on I got involved with Priyom.org, which is...'

I nodded. 'The recording and archiving of Numbers Stations broadcasts. I saw that website when I was Googling this stuff.'

'Indeed. But, in recent years I've been less involved. Once I found out what The Tolworth Beacon's decoding book was. And I know you know it's "The Gathering Hand", I dedicated my time to decoding the broadcasts that came specifically from *that* station. There were various projects or missions going on around the world, all being orchestrated by whoever was controlling the operations behind the Tolworth Beacon. Activities to tweak the outcomes of various environmental or anti-environmental initiatives over the years. I suppose I became more interested because of my parent's involvement in fossil fuels, with all the toxicity, politically and environmentally, that comes with it.'

He took a sip from his bottle of beer, then a drag from his cigarette, smoke escaping as he talked. 'Then about two years ago the broadcasts referenced activities relating to a supermarket in Chalkweald. I decided to take myself a little closer to the action, because, globally speaking, it was on my doorstep. I wanted to see for myself what was going on. But for me it was imperative that I act as a distant observer and not get involved. I rented the house across the street. In that time, two years, I've studied you from over there.'

'You did what?' I couldn't believe what he'd just said. 'You *studied* me?"

'I did.'

'You studied my family? Do you have any idea how bloody sinister that sounds? What the *hell* were...?'

Malcolm held up his hand. 'You never had anything to fear from me. My involvement was only ever completely benign, until, one day I found myself unable to resist. I had a burning desire to dip my toe in the water.'

My phone pinged. I looked at it. It wasn't Steph or her mother. I opened the message. *Mr Powell. Keen to chat about today. We'll pay very well for an exclusive from you. Please reply to arrange a meeting.*

I deleted the text. How did they get my number? I said to Malcolm, 'Why the change of heart? You sent me a jigsaw. Why did you decide to intervene?'

'It was like an addiction. Being so close to something that The Tolworth Beacon was working on but knowing I couldn't touch it. I was completely torn, but like an addict knowing full well that they shouldn't partake, I continued anyway even though I knew it was wrong. By then I knew about The Jigsaw Collective Facebook page. And I saw it as a potential method to quietly deliver information to you without it being noticed by The Tolworth Beacon's operators, who for me were shadows in the background.

Somehow all-seeing. You could say I was giving you the first part of a multi-part message. But after I did it. After I sent you that jigsaw, I knew I'd made a mistake. I reaffirmed to myself that my attempts to inform you about The Tolworth Beacon's plan could destabilise the final outcome.'

'But what outcome? If it was all about today's attack, why didn't the Beacon try to stop the perpetrator? Why let the attack happen?'

'You have a perception of what the Beacon's intentions were, but...'

'It can only have been to harm the Duchess. The Beacon sent the knife man to attack her. Well I stuck it to them!'

My phone pinged again.

Malcolm took one final drag from his cigarette and ground it under his boot. 'Even now there are things I can't tell you, except to say that your assumption about the Beacon's intentions is wrong. Go back through the messages. It will take a while, they go back two years to the beginning of the Chalkweald mission. Once you filter out the messages for other operatives, other missions, you'll see. But whatever you find out, and I know you'll find it, make sure you keep your discoveries to yourself. You'll see why. Keep it to yourself, or all of this will have all been for nothing. To say more now...'

We were silent a while. On the breeze I could hear the distant cars on the bypass. A far-away siren made my heartbeat accelerate. 'I wonder how long Eamonn had been functioning under The Tolworth Beacon's command.'

'At least two years.'

'Not only did he put the effort into changing the layout of the Duchess's route through the supermarket, but he also helped me to get the Store Manager job in the first place. He helped me with my CV and gave me a mock interview. Looking back at it now he may have been instructed by the Tolworth Beacon to help me secure that job. He was certainly quite enthusiastic about it. That was eighteen months ago. But hang on...'

Malcolm grinned. 'You're convincing yourself of the opposite now, aren't you?'

'Without that, without me getting that job I wouldn't have been standing where I was in the line. The man with the knife, the *perpetrator,* may well have got to the Duchess if I hadn't seen him.'

'Don't beat yourself up about the detail now.'

'My daughter is in hospital tonight because of this. I know she was collateral damage but what interest has the Tolworth Beacon got in the Duchess's survival? And why did my daughter have to pay such a price? Did people behind the broadcasts factor *that* into their plans? Or was collateral damage just not a thing for them?'

After a moment Malcolm said, 'I know Eamonn tried to break into my house that night. But I didn't tell the police because we really don't want them poking their noses into this. But I want you to answer a question for me.'

'If I can,' I said.

'Where is he? I know he hasn't turned up for work since Wednesday and I saw the two of you talking outside my house the night before. I was concerned enough that I knew I had to get off the scene immediately. Tell me, he doesn't have a dog, does he?'

'I don't think he does, no.'

'Do you have any idea where he went?'

I was about to lie. I was about to shake my head, but instead I said. 'I don't know how, but he must have triangulated the broadcast to...'

Malcolm clicked his fingers and pointed at me. 'He went to Haleswade Leap. I knew it.'

'Yes but...'

'But Haleswade Leap's a decoy, or a repeater maybe because there's nothing there.'

'I know but...'

'And there's no way to triangulate beyond that location because there's nothing else. The broadcast station isn't easy to find either. I went up there once. It's right off the beaten path and the mast is hidden in the trees. But it's not the source. That's the weird bit. The trail goes cold.'

'Eamonn died up there.'

'Died? Shit! You went up there too?'

'Not with him. I found him. Later. Yesterday.'

'How did you know to go there?'

'I found some of his notes at work.'

'But how did he..?'

'I don't know, it was some sort of strong electro-magnetic force. The door was open. He went too close to the equipment. He had a metal plate in his head. The magnetism… the immense power of it pulled the plate right out. He must have died instantly. I didn't even know he had a metal plate, but now I've bloody well seen it with my own eyes. I don't know. The whole thing. I think it must have maddened him. Doing what he was doing. Like you, maybe like an addiction. He had to move closer to the flame. That's why he went out there that day, on Wednesday when he didn't come to work. He went up there to find out where the broadcasts were coming from. It can only mean he can't have already known. If he had, he wouldn't have needed to go looking. And I'm pretty sure he didn't think he'd walk into some hyper electro-magnetised Faraday cage with a magnet so strong it would kill him.'

'Have you told anyone?'

I shook my head, 'I daren't. Worried I'll be implicated.'

'Did anyone see you there?'

'No people, but there could be CCTV of my car in the area.'

'I somehow don't think people go up to that mast very often. It could be weeks before they find him.'

'I hope you're right.'

Malcolm stood. 'I'm sorry about what happened to your daughter. No child should have to experience anything like that. I'm very sure she'll bounce back stronger.'

'Thank you. Look there's a gate in the fence at the back of the communal gardens. If I switch the security light off by the front door I can sneak you out that way and hopefully no one out front will see you.'

'Sounds like a plan. Lead the way.'

After Malcolm had gone I texted Steph to see how Freya was doing. It was just after ten o'clock.

My phone rang almost immediately. I answered and said, 'Is she awake?' I started walking through the flat to the bedroom.

Steph spoke in an almost whisper. 'No, she's been asleep for about two hours now. Mum went home to pack me an overnight bag, she just dropped it off but now she's gone home. I'm going to get my head down in a bit. I was just looking at all the news on my phone. You and Freya are all over it.'

In the darkness of the bedroom, I pulled the curtains together. 'They're camped outside in the street. Why don't they just go home? I've even had texts from journalists.'

'So have I. How did they get our numbers?'

'Officer Scanlan told me to say nothing for now?'

'He said the same to me and Mum. They think she'll be ok to come out tomorrow.'

'That's fantastic.'

'But... can we come home?'

I was about to tell her she didn't need my permission to leave hospital, but that wasn't what she was talking about was it? She didn't mean that at all.

'Oh my God yes. Yes, I want that if you do.'

I couldn't sleep, so I sat in bed thumbing through "Edmund Tolworth, Collected Poems and Essays 1795-1820" and one particular passage caught my attention. It was in one of his personal essays entitled "Green Earth Black Earth"

I met the entrepreneur Arthur Hollyway at an artist's dinner at London's Guildhall on the twenty first of March 1818. He was young, handsome, and well turned out. I must confess I didn't immediately warm to the man, he came across quite brash at first when I saw him holding court with others. But we were placed together, and I was intrigued to hear him talk about his concerns about the impact of machine processes on the environment. And also, the ways he thought that those that sought to profit from others would need to prepare themselves to be accountable for their impact on the natural world. I too had thoughts on this and once we realised we stood on the same ground on this matter we didn't part company until the carriages.

The essay to me painted a picture where Arthur Hollyway was quite clear about his desire to weave environmental responsibility into the fabric of Hollyways corporate culture, even as long ago as two hundred years. But what of Tolworth? The poem that followed it, entitled "To Times Beyond", written in 1819, was interesting.

Was there ever a time,
When hands would hold green blades,
Up and see,
Ships of the earth climb high,
And take the seeds of us,
And all we share beyond?
Before the blackened wastes,
Of our labour's products pervade,
Through hoodwinked ignorance,
Through melted ice,
Through science scorned,
Through the coins of greed,
I sigh and take the path back,
To plant other seeds,
Not bound by the bonds of Earth.

This second poem seemed prophetic, with its references to "science scorned" and "melted ice". You'd be forgiven for thinking the man had the ability to see through time, based on the words he used.

It was clear from the broadcast messages that were being delivered across the airwaves that The Tolworth Beacon operated on a global level, its oscillations writing themselves into the stone, wood and metal fabric of a whole world of structures, not just the churches, offices and apartment blocks of Chalkweald. There had been another operation ongoing in the Amazon, and the station had been operating for decades. With the Beacon having a global reach, surely it was just a coincidence that Tolworth and Hollyway crossed paths in southern England all those years ago.

These thoughts energised me, gave me a second wind. I got up and went through to the lounge, fired up my laptop and logged onto TOLWORTH-RELAY.NET, which was now functioning normally. I decoded tonight's broadcast. There was nothing for Outcome Calibrator 4316, also known as Eamonn. Did they know he was dead? Or was his work now done? Some other new activity was spinning up near a nuclear power station in Central France. It seemed that in Chalkweald they had achieved what they wanted. They'd calibrated their outcome and were now moving on to other concerns. And soon they would be changing the decoding book.

I went back a week and listened to the broadcast from last Saturday, transcribing the numbers over the course of thirty minutes before spending another hour decoding them using "The Gathering Hand".

*OC4316TRAJECTORYOFPERPETRATORREQUIRESREALIGNMENTT
OENSUREINTERSECTIONWITHTARGETSTOPPATHWAYLENGTHIN
CREASEOFFIVEMETRESNONTIGHTCURVEREQUIREDSTOPSLFSKS
DFJVJKDFALVREUHREIJHGDEQDGHJHBGFGUIOIOJHFGHJFGSHRH
JHGJKLGHJXKLVNZXJCVKZXLNVQPWMCGZRZXNOEJSBSDYCKSNF
JKSCJK*

The hour was late, but I couldn't stop there. I decoded the one from Sunday, just three hours before Eamonn's attempted burglary of Malcolm Renfield's house. The message translated as.

*OC4316INTERVENTIONALERTSTOPMALCOLMRENFIELDIDENTIFI
EDASHAVINGATTEMPTEDTOALERTKEYACTORTOTHISCALIBRATI
ONACTIVITYSTOPATTEMPTINTERVENTIONTOPREVENTDESTABIL
ISATIONOFINTENDEDOUTCOMESTOPHDYSGCFHSDSJFLAHDUEH
DJVKSBJHLSFASBDFUACNCHUAINLTHUGINSLHLVSEYRUQIEWJK
VJVK*

That was an instruction to Eamonn to establish how much Malcolm Renfield knew, which no doubt led to the attempted burglary. Now I needed the one from Monday. The next day. I selected that section of the sound wave on TOLWORTH-RELAY.NET and set about decoding it. I was getting better at it now. Faster. It came out as:

*OC4316ENSUREPROBABILITYMAXIMISEDSTOPWITHPATHWAYAL
IGNEDTHEPRIMARYTARGETWILLINTERSECTWITHPERPETRATOR
STOPENSUREPROBABILITYMAXIMISEDNONCRITICALINJURYLIKE
LYBUTREQUIREDTOENSURECORRECTOUTCOMESTOPJUFDJSKLFS
HJFKLAVNJLFASNNUIQERTWJOCNJSDJKSLNHNLHUGNLDPSENCH
NJLN*

And that was it!

I stood up, scraping the dining chair back. Running my hands through my hair.

That was it! The primary target. I thought it had been the Duchess. But it wasn't. It wasn't the Duchess. I thought it had been me. I would never have guessed it wasn't me either. But it wasn't. It wasn't. It *wasn't*!

SUNDAY

Even at seven in the morning, the sun was making plans to bake the country for another day. I stood in the kitchen drinking a mug of tea and staring at our local star rising from behind the hills beyond Tilmere Woods and shining directly into my eyes. But it was also a sun rising on a world that felt profoundly different, in the same way your home feels different, unable to reconcile itself, after you return from a long time away.

The TV news was on in the lounge. It was talking away to itself about sport.

It had been a text from Steph that woke me. *Freya's still asleep. I haven't got any sleep left in me. The nurses said you can come down anytime, but because there are news people out front we will bring you in a back way so contact us when you get here.*

I replied to say I would get organised and get over there as soon as possible. She replied with, *Bring good coffee!*

I made myself some toast with jam and took it with me into the lounge.

On the TV they kept coming back to the events of yesterday, in between the sport and the weather. The story of a knife attack in a supermarket would be headline news in itself, even though the perpetrator had been stopped, but add in a member of royalty and it's a global event. The scene had been caught on camera from a number of places, which they showed over and over again while people talked. Outside broadcast footage consisted of two main angles. A wide shot taken from high up, either on the broadcast vehicle or near it. The image consisted of the whole scene. The supermarket, the car park, the crowds.

At the moment when the fireworks go off, the camera zooms in to get a closer look. It's impossible to tell who started them. But the police move in quickly to disperse the crowd, which frankly appeared to be doing a pretty good job of dispersing itself. Suddenly, within a cohesive crowd of several hundred people a hole opens up near the entrance, people pushing back as the colour and smoke and bangs and whistles interrupt the normality. According to the news, nobody had been hurt, amazingly.

A closer shot from a handheld camera, also part of the outside broadcast team, initially in place to film the Duchess exiting the car, looks on as she and Dame Hollyway meet the CEO and his wife, the Mayor and the council leader, and then Marianne Evans in her wheelchair before starting to follow the Duchess into the supermarket. Once inside he waits by the door, capturing a wide shot of the proceedings inside. The bunting, the crowds, the cheering, the flags. People pointing their phones and looking at their framing because, why look at something right in front of you when you can look at a smaller version of it, digitised on a five-inch screen. And there's me and Clem, waiting by the plaque as the Duchess walks along our extended route that veered nearer to the fresh produce than was originally planned. I watch myself. Clem and I are looking at the Duchess. From where the camera is I'm unable to see the knife man in his blue shirt or the dropped knife packaging on the floor. But as the Duchess gets to me the camera swings away towards the sound of the fireworks. I thought it had happened later but maybe the rising sound hadn't reached us then. After that the cameraman moved out through the entrance to see what was going on. A closer image of the firework maelstrom. Smoke rising amid the pops and crackles, illuminated pink and red and green. A fire extinguisher, brandished by none other than the tall police officer from the attempted burglary, ensures that the spectacle goes on for less than fifteen seconds. But of course, that meant that the cameraman didn't capture the main event inside.

And then I'm watching mobile phone footage on the screen, which had been taken by a guest inside. There I was, talking to the Duchess and then the mobile phone turns towards the source of the noise outside, and misses what's going on almost right in front of them. By the time they swing the camera back to the action inside, half of it has already happened. The altercation between me and the man had already taken place. The camera wobbles a lot and eventually catches the bastard lying on the ground being subdued by two plain-clothes officers.

Then they were interviewing an ex police officer on the sofa in the television studio, who was saying that that the fireworks outside were no doubt part of a coordinated diversion to allow the knife man inside to make his attack and give him a better chance of carrying out his intentions, which were clearly to harm the Duchess.

The TV presenter stated that some footage was being withheld due to being of a graphic nature.

Yeah, I thought. Footage of my daughter bleeding on the tiles of the nation's favourite supermarket. Not a good advert for the supermarket that prides itself on being "Your family partner for two hundred years".

Then they cut to our Hospital. A female reporter was standing outside the main entrance.

'Thank you. I'm here at Chalkweald Hospital where a young girl was brought in after the events yesterday at Hollyways supermarket. She was caught up in the commotion and was injured. Her name has not yet been revealed by the authorities, but it is known that she is the daughter of a member of staff at Hollyways. Her condition is said to be stable and she is recovering well. Footage of the incident has emerged which shows the man with the knife colliding with the young girl while trying to make a getaway. She is being heralded as a hero for bringing the man down, allowing police officers to restrain him before he could do any further harm. The girl's father is also reported to have deflected the attacker as he made an attempt to get to the Duchess.'

My heart was pumping at that point. Tears of high emotion welling across my eyelids. Pride, and a need to hold my girls. This was going to run and run. And the press weren't going to stop until they got interviews.

◆ ◆ ◆

I received further instructions from Steph as I drew near to the hospital. I used the voice activation on my phone to read the text aloud as I drove. *Drive to the rear staff car park. There's a fire exit there. We have someone waiting there to let you in.*

Pulling into the hospital I caught sight of the crowd of reporters near the entrance. I was able to keep a good distance as I drove around the side of the main building to the staff car park at the rear. I wasted no time getting out of the car and I headed over to the fire exit. A young nurse on the other side opened the door for me and held it open as she saw I had two large coffees in my hands. 'Thank you,' I said to her as the warm outside air gave way to strong, cool, medicinal air as I crossed the threshold of the building.

◆ ◆ ◆

Steph took the coffee with grateful eyes. We hugged for a long time. But it wasn't a hug was it? We were *holding* each other, and there's a difference. It was something I didn't think would happen again. But there it was.

'I have something I need to tell you,' I whispered. 'Something I need to show you. But it can wait till later.'

She looked right at me and said 'Okay.'

I leaned over and kissed Freya on the forehead. I stroked her hair. She had a lot more colour in her cheeks now. She smiled when she wasn't aware of the pain in her arm, but occasionally winced. Her lips were no longer cracked and grey, her hair had been brushed. Jeremy the pink rabbit lay on her chest.

Sophie Dent was also there. She greeted me by saying in a voice intended for Freya 'Mr Powell, your daughter will not stop asking about her operation! She wanted to know everything about what we did. How we fixed her up. She wanted to know all the detail. Soon she'll be able to take her doctors exams and help me out with all my operations!'

Freya giggled. 'Daddy I'm not going to be a lifeguard when I grow up any more. I'm going to be a surgeon!'

'Being here has really captured her imagination. We don't often get that.' Winking at Freya she said. 'She's definitely one to watch this one!'

'Well,' I said, smiling through forming tears. 'Either way you'll be saving lives. And that's alright in my book.'

Sophie Dent touched my elbow. 'Can I have a private word with you both?'

Steph said to Freya. 'We're just going into another room for a few minutes okay?'

Freya nodded.

Officer Tom Scanlan met us in the corridor, carrying his own cup of coffee. He looked like he hadn't had much sleep either. The four of us went into the same room we'd waited in the day before and sat down. There were two more people in there. A young man and an older woman. They stood up as we walked in.

The woman said, 'Mr and Mrs Powell, my name is Jill Ward. I'm a police liaison officer. I'm here to help you over the coming days with some of the attention you are likely to receive, and this is Daniel Ash.'

'Hi. I'm a police media comms liaison. I can coordinate things with the press. You and Freya are going to be in the spotlight for a while and it's important that you are able to respond to that in a healthy way.'

Steph said to Daniel, 'Do we have to pay you?'

Daniel shook his head. 'Not at all. The Crown is taking care of things.'

I said, 'The Duchess.'

'...Is full of gratitude for what you and your daughter did yesterday,' said Jill. 'And she has sent a message that she would very much like to speak with you on the phone and meet with you both in the next couple of days. We can arrange that. But right now, we have to tackle the immediate things in front of us.'

'Like getting your daughter better, and getting her home from the hospital,' said Daniel. 'We all know what the British press are like. They have already worked out who you are, so we may as well release that information and make it official.'

'What about the man?' said Steph.

'The man,' said Jill, 'is in custody, thanks in no small part to your daughter, and although he didn't manage to harm the Duchess, thanks in no small part to *you* Chris, he has been charged with assault and attempted murder.'

'But who is he?' Steph said.

I said, 'He had a swastika tattoo on his arm. I think we know who he...'

'But what's his name?'

'His name is Anthony Woodruff,' said Officer Scanlan. 'He's not been previously known to us. While we've had him in custody he's been sprouting all sorts of nonsense. Denying climate change.'

'And will his name be released to the press too?'

'Not by us, but again, the media are very resourceful, they already know who he is. Thankfully, they've taken the collective view not to name him, not to give him the "oxygen of publicity" as they say, which is a first.'

'How did he get in?' said Steph.

'He was on the guest list.'

'Whose guest was he?' I asked.

'We can't disclose that,' said Jill.

Daniel turned to Sophie, 'What time will you be discharging Freya?'

'Within the hour. I just need to sign some paperwork, and we need to discuss a few things you'll need to know about caring for her over the next few days, then arrange an appointment for her to come back for us to check everything's healing as it should be.'

'So, the question now is. Do you all want to go out the back way, or the front way?' Daniel handed me a piece of paper. 'If you want to go out the front, we've put together a press statement which you can either read out, or I can read it for you.'

◆ ◆ ◆

Steph called Katrina and asked if she could pack Freya's and her things into their cases and bring them to the hospital. 'We can transfer them into our car boot here without the press seeing. Find a way to get them in the flat later. I don't want them thinking we don't live together.'

'I agree,' I said. It felt like the safest option. Give the press only what was necessary. Neither of us wanted them digging into our lives. Like all couples, we wanted to hold onto our secrets.

When the time came to leave Chalkweald Hospital, I carried Freya, with Steph beside me, and we gave them the photograph they had all been waiting for. Daniel read the prepared statement to the crowd.

'We won't be taking any questions today, but we do understand there is considerable national interest in what has happened here. During the situation at the supermarket yesterday a young girl sustained a minor injury. She is healing well and has been discharged from Chalkweald Hospital. This is an ongoing police investigation and we will not be giving out any further detail at this time. Please bear with us while we continue to bring more information to light. Thank you.'

The statement may have been light on detail, but it was the photograph that they wanted. The father and daughter hero team that saved the Duchess and stopped a bad man in his tracks.

She'd been in there, and everyone had waited.

Now we were going home.

◆ ◆ ◆

Steph appeared at the door to the kitchen while Edmund Tolworth's words filled the dining room from my laptop speaker.

On Southern green 'neath bluest heaven,
We met once between rhododendron and birch,
But those scents were not so striking when our embrace,
Connected again between land and sky,
So divine a gift I cannot recreate,
On this field or another,
Because pure yearning disappears,
With the clouding of an ageing province.

'What you up to?' she said.

'Is she asleep?'

'Yes, finally. She keeps talking about how she wants to be a surgeon when she's older. She asked if she has a guardian angel. I have no idea where she got that from.'

It occurred to me that Freya did have a guardian angel, in a way. 'Come here and I'll tell you what I'm up to. I think I need your help.'

'Can I get us a glass of wine first?'

'Of course.'

I told Steph everything. From the jigsaw to everything that happened with Eamonn to the evolving pathway at the supermarket. From the radio broadcasts to "The Gathering Hand" to the messages that were being delivered to Outcome Calibrators the world over. From how I thought the Duchess was the target, to how I thought I was the target, to how I now knew that the real target was in her room right now dreaming of Princesses and Cute Spiders, even though I didn't know why. But there was a way we could know, and it would take time.

Steph listened while I talked, and she was astonished. We finished the bottle and opened another one. And that evening we started the real work. Both of us together. Steph suggested using speech to text transcribing apps on our phones to allow us to record the codes directly from TOLWORTH-RELAY.NET into text files without having to do it manually. I agreed it would be worth testing that approach. We could just leave them to play in another room while we got on with the decoding of other broadcasts. She was much more organised than I was. We had two years' worth of messages to work through. It was a lot of work, but with two of us it would take half the time.

EPILOGUE

Freya spoke into the microphone, addressing the assembled crowd. As she did so she toyed with the augmented reality glasses in her hands, which had aided her progress through the more complicated parts of the operation. 'The procedure was a success. Dr North is awake and alert, but she has a lot of healing to do and there will now be an extended period of recovery. Many months, in fact.'

Her colleague stepped forward. 'As head of the hospital I would personally like to express my gratitude to our most celebrated surgeon, Miss Freya Powell, and her team, who have worked throughout the night to stabilise Dr North. There are not many surgeons in the world who would have been able to carry out this procedure. And none in this country who could have attended so quickly given the urgency of Dr North's situation.'

A reporter asked, 'Is there any sense, Miss Powell that the fall was an indication of an underlying physiological issue.'

'Absolutely not,' said Freya. 'All the tests we have run through the night show that Dr North's brain function was, and is, completely fine. Accidents happen. When someone slips on the stairs, they slip on the stairs, no matter who they are.'

Addressing the hospital head another reporter asked, 'Will Dr North be able to access her encrypted files to compete her work and ultimately present her findings to the Climate Committee? Her aggressive recommendations are expected to delay the impending climate singularity. They've been the source of much speculation, but these recommendations are widely tipped to be the key steps that will reverse the global warming trend for good.'

'Thanks to our team of surgeons, we have every confidence at this stage that Dr North will be able to continue her work. In the face of all adversity, delaying the climate singularity is critical for every living thing on this planet.'

More questions came their way, but now that the primary focus was off Freya, her eyes traversed the room. A few rows back behind the reporters she caught sight of Mum and Dad.

Dad smiling with pride.

After the press conference she embraced them both.

'Freya,' her Dad said. 'Let's go and get some breakfast. Your mother and I have something we've waited thirty years to tell you.'

ACKNOWLEDGEMENTS

I've been planning this novel for a couple of years, but I delayed ever making a start on a first draft, with work and family commitments giving me a reason to procrastinate. The idea of trying to compete the first draft in a month came from the NaNoWriMo initiative. But I also wanted to make it a challenge for charity, a "sponsored write" if you like.

I've seen Cancer affecting lot of people around me and take lives in recent months. Which is why I chose Cancer Research UK as the recipient of donations for my sponsored write. During the leap year month of February 2020 I completed a 36,000 word first draft of the book.

I want to express my heartfelt gratitude to all the people who donated and helped me raise (at the time of writing) over £300 for the charity.

Thanks to Lisa and Gareth Jones, Amanda Curtis, Róisín Lilley, Tony Barber, Ruth Stewart, David Smith, Monika Fried, Rob Ashcroft, Richard Bartley, Simon Jones, Dave Phillips, Liam Johnson, Tony Morgan, Lyn Langridge-Jones, Dave Shepherd, Gerry Holton and Michael Langridge. Plus all those who donated anonymously.

Thank you to my parents for reading a very early first draft and giving me their thoughts.

Thank you also to Gerry Holton for additional editorial comments, and for rightly correcting me on a couple of factual inaccuracies.

I also want to pay a huge debt of appreciation to Barry Brown and also Tony Morgan for giving up their time to provide me with some extremely valuable insight into police process. Any inaccuracies are my own.

And last but not least, my five-year old daughter Martha for first writing out the words "Kyoot Spighdaz", my son Oliver for reading sections of an early draft, and my wonderful wife Alison for putting up with my frantic writing schedule and being the beating heart of our home, especially during the ongoing Coronavirus lockdown.

North Wales
April 2020

ABOUT THE AUTHOR

Huw Langridge

Huw Langridge grew up in London and, during his years working as a global IT troubleshooter for an oil exploration company, he journeyed to a number of places that enabled him to find inspiration and tone for his stories. More recently he has travelled the world working on an operations team delivering high-calibre investment conferences, and managing Major Incidents within Cheshire East Council's IT department.

In July 2003 Huw attended an Arvon Foundation novel-writing course at the residential retreat at Lumb Bank in Yorkshire. The course was tutored by Martyn Bedford ("The Houdini Girl" and "Acts of Revision") and Phil Whitaker ("Triangulation" and "The Face"). The guest author was Louise Welsh ("The Cutting Room"). Also in attendance was Ian Marchant ("Parallel Lines"). Huw has cooked for all of them, and is glad they survived the ordeal.

Huw's first short story publication was the science fiction piece "The Ceres Configuration", published in Issue 4 of Jupiter SF Magazine, released in April 2004. The story was described by Adrian Fry of Whispers of Wickedness as "A good old fashioned (yet high-tech) tale of approaching apocalypse, which served to remind me just what unpretentious science fiction can do when written by someone who clearly relishes every word."

In Autumn 2004 he produced an eNovel called Spireclaw.

Huw released his first print novel Schaefer's Integrity in December 2008 and is available at all major online booksellers. Further published short works have appeared in The Ranfurly Review, Reflection's Edge, Jupiter SF, 365tomorrows and Supernatural Tales.

His short story "Last Train to Tassenmere" received an Honorable Mention in Ellen Datlow's Year's Best Horror 2009.

In September 2010 he released his short story collection The Axiom Few, featuring three previously published stories and five stories new to the collection. His Axiom Few stories have received praise from a number of online SF review websites, such as SF Signal, SF Site and SF Crowsnest.

After his eNovel "Spireclaw" received praise online, Huw decided to release a non-profit print version which came out in September 2011.

Further short story collections include a set of ghost stories entitled "The Train Set" and a book of science fiction shorts called "A Comet of Ideas Looking for a Planet", both available on Kindle.

Huw gets his inspiration from music, travel and the seasons. He lives by the sea in North Wales with his wife and two children.

huwlangridge.blogspot.com
www.twitter.com/huwlangridge

BOOKS BY THIS AUTHOR

The Train Set

Ghosts haunt our railways. Sinister seaside towns lurk at the end of branch-lines not visible on any train map. A dark and disused London Underground station harbours a diabolical secret. Families come together and grow, and families are broken apart.

"The Train Set" consists of six stories.

Two previously published works, "At Steepdean Halt", first published in 2008 in The Ranfurly Review, and "Last Train to Tassenmere" which after its publication in Supernatural Tales received an honourable mention in Ellen Datlow's Year's Best Horror of 2009.

Rounding out the collection are three new short stories, and "Flyers", a brand new novella.

Spireclaw

All the time we are surrounded by coincidences. Some we pay a second thought to and then forget about. Some fill us with wonder. Some we never even notice. But there are some which can scare us. When Kieran Whyteleafe starts to see little coincidences happening around him he decides to investigate their meaning. The coincidences seem to centre around the word Spireclaw. Why does the word keep appearing in places only meant for Kieran's eyes? Is it connected to the suicide of his old school friend?

And what is the significance of the archive boxes that turn up mysteriously at his work. Kieran's desire to solve some of the puzzles that surround him has pitched him on a trajectory of discovery, and his investigations will culminate in a revelation that is too shocking for him to comprehend.

Schaefer's Integrity

Duncan Schaefer is a chef in the Kuiper Mining Colony, at the edge of our solar system. He has become infected by a virus that is baffling science. With the help of his disfigured companion Maxan, he struggles to understand the physical changes his body is undergoing, which is earning him an unwanted celebrity status. Everyone wants a piece of him. Schaefer soon learns that the illness has a design of its own, and that there are greater things at stake than just his own life. Can he survive long enough to uncover the mystery of his illness, and make the connection between the physical changes in his body, and the future of mankind's place in the universe?

The Axiom Few

Archer, Geek and Davey are The Axiom Few, a small band of freelance techno-graduates who operate on the edge of science in a future London. Welcome to the test-shack. This short story collection contains three previously published stories and five that are new to this release.

Reviews of The Axiom Few

"...Come on, Channel 4, there's a series waiting to be made here..." - SFCrowsnest.com

"....A good old fashioned (yet high-tech) tale of approaching apocalypse, this story served to remind me just what unpretentious science fiction can do when written by someone who clearly relishes every word..." - Whispers of Wickedness

"...Beautifully crafted..." Annieworld

"...a nicely told story of alternate realities..." SFRevu

Printed in Great Britain
by Amazon